F
The Dahlonega Sisters Series

"What an absolute pleasure it was to read *The Dahlonega Sisters by Diane M How*. This moving family drama, laced with mystery, is a beautiful, touching romance and a lot more besides *Diane M How* brings to life such wonderful characters that if they were real people, I would love to meet them."

5-star review by Jewel Hart, Editor
Book Marketing Specialist
Author Visibility/Brand Consultant
<u>Chick Lit Cafe-Bookstagram</u>

"You can't help but like these women and you are going to want to get to know them better. Each has their own unique personality and the conclusion wraps it all up in one neat package, although I believe there is a follow-on story. I'm looking forward to reading it. This story will keep you happily immersed in the sisters' world for a few hours."

Congratulations on your 5-star review!
—Reviewed By Anne-Marie Reynolds
for *Readers' Favorite*

I was thoroughly charmed by this story of sisterhood /family, return to faith, small town living, and second chance at love. The main characters (Mutzi, Marge,

Rose Ellen, and April) are all relatable and real. Ms. How gave each of them distinct personalities right from the start with quirks and mannerisms that make them likable and sympathetic.

4.5-star review by Maida Malby, *Carpe Diem Chronicles*

Praise for *The Dahlonega Sisters – The Gold Miner Ring*

"*The Dahlonega Sisters* is such a fun and delightful read, I want to get to know the three sisters in real life." —Jeanne Felfe, author of *Bridge to Us*

"The bond between the Dahlonega sisters is secured by celebrating their differences in the mist of conflict and heartache. The story symbolizes how answers to the past can pave the way for the future not only for these women, but for us all."

—Nicki Jacobsmeyer, Author of *Images of America: Chesterfield*, Arcadia Publishing

"This delightful novel twists and turns with comedy, romance, tugged heart strings, mystery and more. *The Dahlonega Sisters* entertains on every page."

—Tammy Lough, Award-Winning Author and Romance Columnist at DIYMFA.com

To Carolann
My treasured friend

The Dahlonega Sisters

Veins of Gold

~ ✺ ~

Diane M. How

[signature: Diane M. How]

Silver Lining Publishing, L.L.C.

ST. PETERS, MISSOURI

Published by Silver Lining Publishing, L.L.C.
70 Oakridge West Drive
St. Peters, Missouri 63376 (United States of America)

Publisher's Note: This is a work of fiction. Names, characters, places, and incidents are a product of the author's imagination. Locales and public names are sometimes used for atmospheric purposes. Any resemblance to actual people, living or dead, or to businesses, companies, events, institutions, or locales is completely coincidental. Although some real-life iconic places are depicted in settings, all situations and people related to those places are fictional.

Book Layout © 2017 BookDesignTemplates.com
Book Editing and Formatting by Jeanne Felfe
Cover Design by Jennifer Quinlan of Historical Editorial
Cover Photos: iStock and Adobestock

Publisher's Cataloging-in-Publication Data
provided by Five Rainbows Cataloging Services

Names: How, Diane M, 1951- author.
Title: The Dahlonega sisters : veins of gold / Diane M. How.
Description: St. Peters, MO : Silver Lining Publishing, 2020. | Series: Dahlonega sisters, bk. 2.
Identifiers: LCCN 2020922179 (print) | ISBN 978-1-7340383-3-0 (paperback) | ISBN 978-1-7340383-2-3 (ebook)
Subjects: LCSH: Sisters--Fiction. | Family secrets--Fiction. | Older women--Fiction. | Women--Fiction. | Georgia--Fiction. | Small cities--Fiction. | Humorous stories. | BISAC: FICTION / Family Life / Siblings. | FICTION / Women. | FICTION / Humorous / General. | FICTION / Southern. | GSAFD: Humorous fiction. | Love stories.
Classification: LCC PS3608.O8965 D341 2020 (print) | LCC PS3608.O8965 (ebook) | DDC 813/.6--dc23.

This book is dedicated to an amazing woman, a brilliant writer, and my dear comrade, Jeanne Felfe. From the time we first met in a critique group, she has nurtured, instructed, and encouraged me to become a better writer. Besides being an excellent editor, she makes herself available to everyone who needs guidance and asks for help. This intelligent, strong, and unselfish woman also serves as President of Saturday Writers, perhaps the best writing club in Missouri, devoting endless hours to the success of the organization and expecting nothing in return. My heartfelt thanks to Jeanne. You are a treasured friend.

Dahlonega, Georgia

It really isn't hard to say once you've tried it a few times. You don't need to roll your eyes or thump your forehead, but it might help to get started.

Duh lon eh ga

Duh lon eh ga

One more time. Duh lon eh ga

You've got it!

This quaint, historical town is in Northeast Georgia and is the first official gold rush location in the United States. Bet you thought that happened in California. Wrong.

Visitors from across the nation are attracted to Dahlonega because of the friendliness of the folks living there and the exciting events they sponsor, like the annual Gold Rush Festival held each October.

Right in the middle of their bustling town square is the Dahlonega Gold Museum. There are too many other attractions to mention here, but one of my favorites is the Consolidated Gold Mine where visitors can pan for gold or sift through buckets for hidden gems.

The town of Dahlonega is real, as are many of the locations mentioned in Veins of Gold. However, everything else is fictional. The McGilvray sisters, Marge, Mutzi, and Rose Ellen, are pretend characters. **All the events/scenes** in Veins of Gold only took place in my imagination.

I hope you fall in love with The Dahlonega Sisters and their lovely town. If you're looking for a new adventure where you can pan for gold, kayak down the Yahoola Creek, and nibble on scrumptious chocolate while sipping delicious wine, add Dahlonega, Georgia to your schedule. You won't be sorry.

Chapter One

Marge Ledbetter steadied her hand within an inch of the keyboard. She drew in a deep breath, gathered her courage, and with a trembling finger, pressed send.

"You did it."

The unexpected voice startled her. She pivoted toward the door, bumping the desk and launching her wireless mouse across the room.

Ashley McDougal bent to retrieve the gadget. "I can tell by the look on your face. You ordered the DNA kit, didn't you?" Unruly shoulder-length strawberry-blond curls did little to hide the playful smile lighting the teenager's freckled face. "Good for you."

Marge massaged the muscle cramping in her neck. "I can't believe you talked me into this." She rotated her shoulders in exaggerated circles in an attempt to release the tension. "I hope I don't regret it." *What if I'm opening the proverbial can of worms? What if...no, no, don't think like that.*

Ashley tilted her head, soft tendrils brushing her pink cheeks. "There's nothing to be afraid of, Ms. Marge." She moved closer and placed a consoling hand on Marge's shoulder. "My professor says people do it all the time. It'll be okay."

Oh, the innocence of youth. Marge released a sigh and turned off the computer. Scooting the desk chair back, she stood and adjusted her rose flowered apron. "Let's keep this our little secret for now. I'm not sure how my sisters feel about digging into our ancestors' past."

Ashley placed a slender finger on her lips and her blue eyes drifted toward the ceiling as if deep in thought. "I really like your twin, Mutzi. She's funny and always shares interesting information. I can't wait to meet—Rosie—no, that's not it. Rose Ellen, your older sister.

"I'm surprised you remembered she likes to be called by her proper name. She's been traveling for so long, I didn't realize you haven't met her."

"I haven't, but hearing you and Mutzi talk about her makes me feel like I know her." She tipped her head. "I wonder if my sisters will be as close as you three are after we graduate. Hope so. I can't imagine being apart from them."

Marge tended to forget Ashley was a freshman in college. Her joyful, light-hearted spirit made her seem much younger than her two triplet sisters. The three girls had filled a purposeful need when Mutzi moved out and left her with an empty house and too much time on her hands. "I imagine you will all have some times when you go your separate way. But they're your family and you'll always cherish the special bond and memories you've made, even if you're far away."

"I believe we remember things that are most important to us. Chelsea knows all the famous artists and designers. I couldn't tell you one painting from another, but she identifies them in an instant."

"I didn't know that about her. Mutzi spent a lot of time studying art, too." Marge pulled a dust cloth from her apron pocket and wiped the credenza.

"Brandi loves buildings and sports. Seems like a weird combination. I've never been good at those kind of things."

"You're good at other things. Everyone has their own talents and interest."

"You're right." Ashley paused and tilted her head. "For me, it's people I've met and recipes. I'm pretty good at those two, but that doesn't help me in my macroeconomics class." She giggled. As Ashley walked around the room looking at the shelves of books and family pictures hanging on the wall, she continued. "My dream is to get married and have a large family." She pointed to one of the photos. "I hope I find a man as special as George. You must miss him, but at least you still have this beautiful Victorian house he bought for you and lots of great memories."

"I do." Marge lingered as she gazed at his picture. *Could it really be ten years now?* She kept busy enough in the daylight hours to ignore the emptiness in her soul, but at night, she longed to be wrapped in his comforting embrace. Many tear-stained pillows had been discarded after serving to ease the fierce ache that consumed her nights.

"This house felt pretty empty when Mutzi left. I wasn't sure if I could stay here all alone. You girls were a God-send."

"Aw, thanks. But *we* are the lucky ones. We all wanted to stay together, but they couldn't accommodate us in the dorms. You were nice enough to offer your home. It's funny how things work out sometimes."

Marge smiled as she glanced from George to Ashley and back again. "Yes it is. It's almost like I had a guardian angel watching over me."

Ashley's eyes grew wide. "I believe in angels too. Is George yours?"

Marge stared at her husband's picture. "I'm pretty sure he is." She glanced at the young woman and smiled. "I guess you've heard me talk to him."

A sheepish grin made Ashley's face light up and she shrugged as she nodded. "I have. But I didn't want to say anything. Does he ever talk back?"

The earnest question triggered an unexpected chuckle from Marge. "Not out loud, but he has his ways."

"Like what?" She clasped her hands together as if anticipating more. "Tell me some of the things he's done."

Marge smiled. "Well, you coming to live here, for one. I had talked with George and told him how empty the big old house was by myself. No more than I finished bemoaning to him, Ms. Brown, the Director of Resident Life at the college, called and said they weren't able to house the three of you. It was like George sent you my way." She placed a hand on her chest and sighed. "He watches over me."

"That is so cool. I want to hear more. Tell me another one."

As much as Marge wanted to go on, she knew they both were on a schedule. "Later. Right now, we need to get baking."

Marge turned and walked into the hall, stopping at the mirror to check her hair before heading to the sun-filled kitchen. She lifted a blue smock from a metal hook hanging on the wall, and handed it to Ashley.

"Did you buy a new apron?

"Not recently. I found it when I was cleaning yesterday. I bought it years ago for Mutzi but she didn't use it very often."

Ashley slipped the loop over her head and stroked the crisp cotton material. "It's so pretty."

"I thought it was, but it didn't have enough pizazz for my sister. She likes bold, bright colors...with busy patterns."

"I noticed she has a unique style. Does she like to cook, too?"

"No." Marge pressed her lips tight remembering a near disaster. "You know how you feel about economics? Well, let's just say Mutzi's skills weren't in the kitchen." Marge shrugged her shoulders. "My sister has many talents, but baking isn't one of them. She nearly burnt down my house once."

"Oh, no. Really? That would have been awful. It's such a perfect place, especially the kitchen." Ashley glanced around. "I love all the decorative touches, like that apple and flower hook. It's so unique and looks like it was made for that space."

"George spoiled me rotten. Worked two jobs to save enough for the down payment on this house. He never forgot a birthday or anniversary." Marge reached out and stroked the ornamental piece. "He insisted on buying this lavish decoration even though it broke our budget. When I told him we couldn't afford it, he said he'd give up cigarettes in order to pay for it."

"Wow. That's amazing. So romantic. How long did he quit?"

"Never smoked another one, for which I was very grateful. He was a special man." Marge released a slow sigh and smiled. "We better get started on those pies."

"Ready and willing. I think I've mastered all the crock pot and stove top recipes you've shown me. I'm ready for something more challenging." Ashley did a pirouette making the pastel blue material float away from her petite body.

She might be eighteen, but she's still a child at heart. Marge had to admit, Ashley was her favorite of the triplets who had come to board with her. She was by far the most domesticated and often offered to help. Her interest in learning to cook was an added bonus.

While all the girls expressed gratitude for Marge providing them housing, Ashley genuinely appreciated not being on campus and spending time with Marge. The grandmotherly connection seemed to fill a void in both of their hearts.

Withdrawing a canister from the pantry, Marge handed it to Ashley. "I thought we'd make two apple, one cherry, and two pumpkin. How's that sound?"

Marge pointed a finger toward the kitchen counter before gathering more items.

"Scrumptious. Too bad they're for the Dahlonega Woman's Club bake sale. They're all my favorites." Ashley tilted her head and asked, "You and Mutzi belong to the club, right?"

"Right."

"I'm curious. What do you use the money from the sale for?"

"It goes back to the community for education. Scholarships, the library, special events for children, those kind of things.

"That's cool."

"Yes it is. They are a wonderful bunch of generous and hard-working women. I'm proud to be part of the group." Marge scanned her eyes over the island to make sure she had everything they needed. Part of it was filled with containers, five pie plates, and a tattered cookbook. She'd placed matching sets of measuring cups, spoons, rolling pins, and knives near the middle.

Ashley's eyes widened as she took it all in. "I had no idea how much stuff it takes to make a few pies. Mom just buys them from a bakery."

"Your mother's very busy with the family business. I doubt she has the time or energy to bake." Marge scrubbed her hands and wiped them on a towel.

"Don't forget to wash first. It's the most important thing to remember when you're going to be handling food."

"Right," Ashley lathered her hands and continued, "I learned that my freshman year in high school." She scoffed, raising her brows with a sideways glance at Marge. "And you remind me every time I help you cook."

"Sorry. I guess I do. I'll have to work on that."

"No prob." Ashley looked down at the smock. "I made a sundress once." She stopped short. "Hey, this is the same color, aquamarine—like my eyes—you're supposed to wear colors that bring out the beauty of your eyes."

Marge couldn't help but laugh. Everything this girl did, she did with enthusiasm. "That's very true and blue is definitely right for you."

Ashley picked up a rolling pin and spun it. "People say I have my dad's eyes." She tilted her head and looked at Marge. "Whose eyes do you have? Your mother's or father's?"

The question made Marge pause. Although most of the photos she'd seen of her mother were black and white, she remembered the portrait of her mom Rose Ellen had taken with her when she moved to New York. How she wished she looked like her beautiful mother.

With a sigh, she responded, "I have my father's."

Ashley scrunched her mouth and drew in her brows. "You sound disappointed. But, you have very pretty brown eyes."

"Thanks." She nodded toward the study. "George called me his brown-eyed girl." The memory brought a smile. Still, she longed to see a hint of her mother's high cheeks and perfectly shaped nose when she looked in the mirror, especially as the years passed and memories of her mother faded. There was one feature she'd never forget. "Emeralds appeared inferior next to my mother's eyes."

"Wow. That's cool. How old were you when she passed?"

"Mutzi and I had started kindergarten—so we just turned five. We came home from school and Daddy told us Mommy went to Heaven." Marge opened the flour canister and paused. "In some ways, it's good we were so young and didn't understand. Later, when we were older, we learned she had an ectopic pregnancy."

A pout made Ashley's bottom lip extend. "That's so sad."

"Enough reminiscing. We've got to get these pies in the oven." Marge held up the measuring cup. "Two cups flour, one cup shortening, and a teaspoon of salt."

Ashley repeated the process as she measured each item with precision.

When she finished, Marge picked up a pastry cutter. "Now you chop it until it gets crumbly." The two of them worked the crust components in silence. Marge stabbed at the mixture, occasionally checking on Ashley's progress.

Realizing Marge was watching, Ashley held up her bowl. "How am I doing?"

"Almost there. See the little globs of white. Blend those in and you'll have it."

"You're a very good teacher." Ashley continued to focus on cutting in the shortening. "It must have been difficult to grow up without your mother."

"We had Rose Ellen—she's five years older than Mutzi and me. She hated cooking—and housework—but she did the best she could. We were too young to know the difference." Marge poured a half cup of ice water into her mixture. "Grandma Dot took care of us when Dad was working. She loved to cook. Guess that's where I learned to enjoy it."

"I wish I had a grandmother who liked to bake. Both of mine are business women like my mom. They send money for our birthdays, but it's not the same."

"Daddy spoiled us with lots of gifts and clothes. Rose Ellen and I loved to dress up, but Mutzi hated anything frilly. I think Daddy tried to compensate for

Mom's absence, but we did okay. That was a long time ago."

"My dad could never have raised us without my mother."

"He might have. You never know what you can do until you try. I'm sure my father doubted he could raise three girls, but he managed somehow."

"I guess. Daddy's always so busy. He would have hired a nanny." Ashley put the pastry cutter down, pausing as if to contemplate the idea. "He probably wouldn't have been able to tell us apart."

"Now that might have taken a little extra effort, for sure. All three of you look so much alike. As infants, it would have been difficult. It's easier now that you each have a different cut and style of your hair, but I bet it was difficult when you were first born."

"I guess." Ashley stared at Marge. "It's funny. Your twin doesn't look anything like you."

The statement brought Marge to a halt. She'd heard the whispers most of her life. "No. I guess she doesn't. It's funny how that happens sometimes." An unwelcome angst stirred in her stomach. Marge tried to ignore the uneasiness by focusing on the pies.

"Sprinkle flour on the marbled island like this." Once Ashley followed her lead, Marge scooped the dough out of the bowl and formed a large ball.

"Now press the mound with your palm, like this. Be gentle but firm. If you knead it too much, it will get tough. Then roll it out into a circle using the rolling pin."

Marge worked the dough, her mind trailing back to Ashley's comment. Ever since she could remember, people questioned how two sisters—much less twins—could look and act so different. For years, she'd refused to entertain their suggestions her sister had been adopted or switched at birth, and at least most days she tried to ignore the comments.

"Miss Marge?" Ashley pointed to Marge's crust. "Is it supposed to look like that?"

Marge looked down at the massacred heap. "Nope. That's my lesson on how NOT to make the perfect pie crust." She gathered the shredded pieces and tossed them into the trash can. "Lesson one. Don't get distracted."

Ashley pointed to her own pastry circle. "How's this?"

"Perfect. Maybe you should be teaching me."

Ashley stared at Marge and drew her brows tight. "Something's bothering you. Want to talk about it?"

Marge pressed her lips tight. "Thanks, but you needn't worry about me. You're much too young to have to manage other people's concerns."

A pained look crept across Ashley's face. "I may not always act like an adult, but I'm good at listening." She fiddled with the dough with downcast eyes. "And I know more than people give me credit for."

"I didn't mean to offend you. I don't like to burden others with my problems."

"But it's important to share your thoughts, especially when you're troubled."

Marge gazed at her protégé. If she'd had a daughter of her own, she'd want her to be just like Ashley, wise and considerate. "You're right. I appreciate your offer. For now, let's finish these pies and get them baking. You've got class soon, and I've got some errands to run."

"All right. But remember, I'm here for you, if you want to talk." Ashley gently lifted the dough and placed it in the pie plate. After she added the fragrant sugar and cinnamon-coated apples, she asked, "What now?"

"I'm going to show you how to make a lattice crust for the top."

"Yum. My favorite."

Marge walked Ashley through the process of crisscrossing the strips of pie dough, then crimping the edges and brushing the final product with an egg wash. When they finished, she placed the pie in the oven along with the one she'd made. "I can finish the rest of these. You better get ready for your class."

Ashley washed her hands and dried them, then stepped next to Marge and placed a hand on her shoulder. "I know what's bothering you." Ashley's mouth formed a tight line. "It's the DNA kit you ordered. You're afraid of what you'll find out."

Marge's pulse quickened. The young woman's words couldn't be closer to the truth if she'd have spoken them herself. "You're too wise for your age, Ashley."

Chapter Two

Sun filtered through the wooden blinds as Samuel Parks zipped his suitcase and set it on the bedroom floor. He glanced in the mirror and smoothed a strand of errant gray hair, taking one last look around to ensure he hadn't forgotten anything.

The small wheels rumbled as he pulled the travel bag behind him down the hallway and idled it near the kitchen door. The tantalizing smoky scent of bacon still lingered from their morning breakfast.

Mutzi finished drying the last of the dishes and set the towel down as Sam walked in. She looked up at him with joyless eyes and a frown accenting her aging face.

"This is wrong." She folded her arms tight against her chest. "I should be going with you, Sam. I'm your wife and you shouldn't have to do this by yourself."

Sam lifted her chin with his curled index finger, placed a kiss on her trembling lips, and then drew her close. "We've talked about this, sweetheart. The logistics won't work, my love." He shook his head. "I wish you could be there with me. But it doesn't make sense for you to sit around for days while they're working on my leg. At least here you have family and friends to do things with."

She pressed her lips tight and looked away. "It's my fault. You married an imbecile...at least the second time."

The comment stung, a reminder that he'd waited more than fifty years to return to the woman he'd always loved. They were childhood sweethearts, planning to marry when he returned from Vietnam. She'd wanted lots of children, and so did he.

The bomb that took his leg also took his manhood—and any chance of fathering children. Angry, depressed, and refusing to ruin her life too, Sam stopped answering her letters, letting her believe he'd died, hoping she'd find another man who could give her the family she wanted and deserved.

When the Army reassigned Sam as a chaplain and sent him to Korea, he met Song. She'd been abused by an American soldier and left behind, like damaged goods. Seen as a disgrace by her family, she was desperate for help and Sam offered her refuge. They'd lived as husband and wife until cancer took her life.

Song knew the depth of Sam's love for Mutzi and encouraged him to return to Dahlonega to find her. Even though he still believed setting his true love free was the right decision, he knew how deeply he'd hurt her. Now, he stirred sadness in her again, but it couldn't be helped.

"I married two smart women, one of whom encouraged me to return to the one I've always loved."

"How many women don't know how to drive? Just me." She released a heavy sigh.

Sam squeezed her tight, stroking her silver hair. He decided to tell Mutzi the truth. "Song didn't drive either." He hoped mentioning her name wouldn't make Mutzi feel worse.

"Really?" She looked up at him as he nodded.

"I never needed to before we got married. If I wanted to go somewhere, I walked to town or my sister drove me." She buried her head into Sam's chest. "All these years without you, you'd think I'd be used to being alone."

"I'll miss you, honey. If you want, when I get back, I'll teach you to drive."

"If we wait a little longer, maybe we can get one of those cars that drives itself." Mutzi chuckled and squeezed Sam tighter.

"It's only for a few days. I promise." He gazed at the woman who measured nearly a foot shorter than him. His heart ached to see her so sad. Tucking a strand of hair behind her ear, he reminded her, "I'll be back Wednesday evening, if everything goes well."

The timing wasn't good, but he had no choice. The foam socket lining of his prosthesis had deteriorated to the point he could no longer stand the pain. It was time to have it replaced. They'd just begun their life together after decades apart. She'd adjusted to the changes and seemed to feel secure with him, but he wasn't sure how she would do with him gone.

Mutzi's eyes widened. "They better make everything right or they'll have to answer to me." She jabbed a thumb into Sam's chest.

Sam took her hands in his. He had no doubt this spitfire woman would give them hell if things didn't go well. "Please don't worry. It'll be fine. I've dealt with worse things."

Mutzi nodded. "Yeah. That's what you say, but you won't tell me about those things."

Knowing what she meant, Sam closed his eyes and shook his head. "Not today, Mutzi. It's time for me to hit the road." He tried to move toward the door, grabbing the handle of his suitcase.

Mutzi stood firm, refusing to release his other hand. "I wish you'd tell me what happened while you were there."

Sam closed his eyes and drew in a deep breath. "Vietnam's not a subject that I want to talk about with you, or anyone else. What happened there"—Sam paused and released a sigh—"let's leave it there."

Mutzi pressed her lips tight. "I don't like it, but I'll respect your wishes. For now."

Hoping to lighten Mutzi's mood and perhaps his own, Sam teased, "Try to behave yourself while I'm gone."

Playing along, Mutzi forced a laugh. "Where's the fun in that?" She held open the kitchen door. "Marge wants me to set up some files on her computer. She's coming by to get me in a little while. Maybe we'll stop at a bar and get drunk. That'd be fun." She gave Sam a devilish grin. "Once I'm in town, I've got all kinds of places to go to get in trouble."

Sam smiled. Mutzi liked her beer, but he knew she'd never get Marge Ledbetter to step a foot in a bar. "See you Wednesday, my love...my forever love." Sam knew the words would linger long after he drove away. They were the last words he spoke to her when he left for Nam.

He tossed his luggage into the back of his truck and strained to climb into the cab. As he secured his seatbelt, Mutzi stood at the door watching him. He blew a final kiss toward her. She reached out and caught the imaginary object, tucking it into the pocket of her bright purple bird-covered smock. Sam couldn't suppress the smile that tugged at his cheeks. He felt like a teenager again every time he looked at Mutzi, save the constant ache in his left leg.

Putting the truck in gear, he drove down the long, black-topped driveway and headed toward Gainesville, already missing her.

Chapter Three

Bright yellow pansies lined the terraced landscape of the pristine two-story. A sense of nostalgia filled Mutzi's heart as she and Marge pulled into the driveway. She'd called the place home most of her adult life, thanks to the generosity of her sister and brother-in-law, George. Mutzi missed the daily routine of hiking into town and shopping in the square, although she had to admit, as she'd aged, the return trip up—which she jokingly named "cardiac hill"—had often left her winded. Still, she treasured the memories they'd made in Dahlonega.

Marrying Sam and moving out of her sister's house had tested Mutzi's courage. While she normally didn't care what others thought, moving in with a man certainly gave the gossip girls something to talk about. Not wanting to have a failed marriage, she needed a trial period to see if she would make the adjustment.

Sam understood her limitations and made the move as effortless as possible. He decorated a separate bedroom for her to stay in until they were married. The "babe cave" he'd designed for her looked just like the one she'd seen on the internet. Even though Sam preferred earth tones, he'd added splashes of bright, cheerful colors to every wall to satisfy Mutzi's vibrant style.

Most important, he'd helped her release many of the superstitions that had previously ruled her life. She no longer feared having her picture taken with her sisters, or eating tomatoes on Tuesday, along with a thousand other silly notions she'd come to believe.

"Place looks really nice, Sis."

"Thanks. Ashley helped me plant the flowers, she's such a delight to have around."

When Mutzi reached the top step of the wrap-around porch, she let out a hardy laugh. "A purple swing? I can't believe it."

Marge shrugged, the hint of a smile lifting the corner of her lips. "Magical Lilac, according to Brandi. She surprised me last week." Marge studied the swing. "It wouldn't have been my choice, but the color's growing on me."

"Purple's a visible wavelength of electromagnetic energy."

"It almost matches your smock. Love the little birds." Marge held open the door, waiting for Mutzi to step into the foyer. "I miss hearing all the bits of knowledge you've got stored in your head, just waiting for the right moment to share them. You never cease to amaze me."

"Lots of things on the internet, waiting to entertain you when you're ready." Mutzi noted a collection of books sitting on the hallway table. A new wooden coat rack anchored one wall and held a rose-colored cashmere Pashmina. With a nod to the changes, her head darted toward the kitchen. "I smell cinnamon rolls. Where are they?"

Marge rolled her eyes and shook her head. "That didn't take long. In the microwave. I saved a couple for you. The girls are pretty fond of them, too."

"How about a cup of coffee before we start on your computer lessons?"

"Sounds good. You know where everything is. I need to put my purse in my room and I'll be right back."

Mutzi had been worried about her sister living alone, but the addition of the college triplets resolved her concerns. Marge seemed to have adjusted just fine.

With the coffee brewing, Mutzi set two plates on the kitchen island and pressed a button on the micro-wave to rewarm the rolls for a few seconds. By the time Marge returned, the coffee was ready and the two sisters sat down.

Marge lifted her steamy mug. "I'm so glad you decided to stay here for a couple of days while Sam is gone."

The mention of Sam's name stirred a hint of regret. Mutzi released a small groan. "I really wish I could have gone with him. I should have been able to drive him."

Marge reached across the marble countertop and touched Mutzi's hand. "I know it's hard, but sometimes it's good to have a few days apart. Makes the heart grow fonder."

"Yeah. The man really gets on my last nerve, being so nice to me all the time." Mutzi smirked. "Really, Sis, I'm looking forward to spending some time with you. I miss our talks, even our sister-fussing. Can't wait to walk into town to see the old familiars." She chuckled as the thought of walking back to the house hit her. "Not sure how much I miss that damn—oops—darn hill."

"You can always call me and I'll come pick you up."

"Not a chance. I'm not letting it conquer me. Not that old yet." Mutzi devoured the delectable roll, licking her finger to get the last drip of icing from it. "You're still the best cook in town, Sis." She gathered the empty plates and washed them along with her sticky hands.

Marge stood and picked up their cups, placing them in the sink. "Far from the best, but I do okay." She rinsed and towel dried them, placing them back in the cabinet.

Mutzi grinned and rubbed her hands together. "Where's this new laptop?"

"On George's desk. I didn't think he'd mind me using his office."

"Pretty sure he wouldn't." Mutzi led the way into the study and looked up at George's picture. "He's proud of you, aren't you, George?" Mutzi turned to Marge and winked. "By the way, he said to start calling it *your* desk."

Marge laughed. "It'll take some practice, but I'll work on it." Marge pulled out the desk chair for Mutzi to sit.

"Nope. I'll get a chair from the dining room. You need to sit in front of the computer. I'll walk you through it, step by step. Promise."

Marge picked up a pen and pad of paper. "I think I'll take notes. I get pretty confused with all the terminology and knowing what keys to press."

"Before long, you'll be creating recipe books and selling them on your own website."

"Maybe we should start with something a little smaller, like creating a document and teaching me how to find it once I've saved it."

The next hour flew by as Mutzi helped Marge experiment with the internet, showing her how to use the voice activation to search and find answers to problems she might encounter.

"Ashley set up an email account for me and showed me how to get to a couple of sites."

"Looks like you've got the hang of the basics. Let's try creating your first document." Mutzi explained how to open the program and name the file.

Ding. Mutzi recognized the familiar sound coming from the speaker.

Marge frowned. "What'd I do wrong?"

"Nothing." In her best imitation of a late nineties movie, Mutzi announced, "You've got mail. Click on that button to see who it's from."

Marge moved the mouse and exposed the message.

When Mutzi saw the startled look on her sister's face, she leaned in closer and began reading. "The DNA kit you requested is on the way?" She jerked her head toward Marge. "What the hell?"

Marge's face turned bright red. "I...I ordered one."

Mutzi jumped from her chair. "Why? Why would you do that?"

"Now, Mutzi. Don't be upset." Marge stood, placing a hand on Mutzi's shoulder. She stammered before continuing. "Ashley's studying ancestry. She's got me interested in learning about our family tree."

"Our family tree? See that big oak in the front yard, that's our family tree."

"But, there's so much more we don't know about our ancestors."

"I already know all I need to know." Mutzi stormed out the front door and down the steps, already knowing things would never be the same once Marge took the test.

Chapter Four

For the third day, Sam watched the distressed man from his hospital window, which faced the Veteran's Administration Medical Center's parking lot. Same faded plaid flannel shirt and worn denims, same forlorn distant stare each time he exited the battle-worn sedan. Sam's years as an Army chaplain, and then a counselor, made it easy for him to recognize homelessness. It pained him to watch the man.

"You're ready, Mr. Parks. We need to go over the discharge instructions."

Sam turned from the window. His mind stirred with thoughts of how to help the man. "Do you know him—the fellow out there?"

The nurse glanced up briefly, her eyes answering before words left her lips.

"Another sad casualty of military life. Can't say anything more." She sighed and returned her attention to the paperwork, holding the pen toward Sam.

He obliged without further questions. Patient privacy rules. He knew them well from his Army career as a chaplain. Not being able to share personal information complicated getting soldiers the help they needed sometimes, but he understood the necessity of it.

He listened while the nurse went into detail, pointing at the papers as she spoke. When she finished, he scribbled his signature. "Good for another three years or ten thousand miles?"

The nurse chuckled. "Can't promise you that, but let's hope your new leg lasts a long time. I'll get someone to roll you out to the curb."

"Don't bother. You're all busy and I need to test out my balance."

"I'm not supposed to let you do that, but we are really short-handed today. Are you sure?"

"I've got this. I'll slip out of here when no one's looking."

When she left the room, Sam checked the hallway. Finding it empty, he grabbed the handle of his suitcase and made his way to the parking lot. Instead of going straight to his truck, he walked toward the battered sedan with the lanky, middle-aged man leaning against it.

Their eyes met. Sam smiled and nodded. "I'm looking for a good place to have breakfast. Any suggestions?"

Cautious dull green eyes stared back, making no effort to accept the extended hand.

The stranger remained leaning against the car, took a drag of his cigarette, and blew a billow of smoke. He shifted his eyes to the left and cleared his throat. "Second Street Diner."

Sam paused. "Thanks. I need something before hitting the road. Heading to Dahlonega."

A hint of interest flickered in the man's eyes, yet his face remained stoic.

An instinct urged Sam to continue. "My truck's right over there. Want to join me?"

The man snubbed out his cigarette and put the remains in his pocket. "Naw." An unmistakable growl came from the stranger's stomach.

Pride. Foolish pride. A man's worst enemy at times like this. Sam continued, "I really hate eating alone. My treat."

The hesitant fellow coughed up phlegm, hocking a gob onto the asphalt, as another rumble from his mid-section followed the offer. "Guess I could eat something." He tried to open his car door, but it refused to budge. He stretched an arm through the partially open window and pulled on the handle. With a loud creak it released and the fellow climbed in. "Meet you there."

Sam made a sharp turn toward his truck and the rushed movement made him grab his knee, reminding him of the reason he was in Gainesville. The pain in his stump, though less severe than when he drove to the center, caused him to grimace as he limped across the parking lot. He tossed the suitcase into the back and eased into the driver's seat, releasing a held groan before turning the key and taking off.

The rusty blue car came into view within a few blocks. Sam found a parking space and ambled into the diner. The pungent odor of stale smoke and musty clothes led him to the stranger now settled in a nearby booth.

Once again, Sam offered his hand to the fellow. "Sam Parks."

The man reached across the table reciprocating. "Chuck—Chuck Hansen."

His cold, boney hand revealed callouses and scars, but not the yarns of how he earned them. Sam studied the aging fellow's whiskered face, trying to imagine the dark path which drove him to this point in his life. His gut told him there was a man worth saving behind the crusty core shielding him. He hoped to gain Chuck's trust and learn his story. Perhaps he could help him in some way.

A heavily endowed blonde wearing a snug white top under her crisply pressed checkered apron neared the booth. She wrinkled her nose and covered it with one hand. With the other she offered a single menu to Sam. "What would you like?"

"Coffee, black." He pointed at the menu. "What's today's special?" Sam met the woman's hard glare.

"Two eggs, hash browns, three slices of bacon, and toast. The super special comes with sausage and grits."

"I'll have the special."

The woman reached for the menu, refusing to acknowledge the other man in the booth.

Sam deliberately handed the menu to Chuck, drawing an eye roll from the waitress. "What do you want, Chuck? My treat. Choose whatever you'd like."

The corner of Chuck's lips lifted his cheeks a smidge, the closest hint of a smile Sam had seen from him so far. "Coffee with two creams and the super special." He held up the menu to her.

The waitress scribbled the order on her notepad, then snatched the menu and marched off toward the kitchen.

Chuck fiddled with his napkin and silverware, then muttered, "Can't blame her for hating the likes of me." His head dropped and shoulders slumped. "Just look at me."

Sam rested his elbows on the table and clasped his hands together. "Hate's a pretty strong word. Maybe she's having a bad day. Never know what people are going through until you get to know them."

Chuck nodded as he looked away toward the window. "True. So true."

As the waitress returned with their coffees, another customer called out to her for a refill. "Hold your horses, Baxter. I'll get you in a minute." She plopped the mugs on the table, spilling some of their contents in the process. "Shit." Her eyes brimmed with unshed tears.

Chuck grabbed a napkin and tried to soak up the mess. "Rough day? Looks like they're working you pretty hard."

The tight lines encircling her blue eyes eased as she grabbed a towel and finished drying up the mess she'd made. "We're short-handed. I should be home with my two-month old—he was up all night sick. My piece-of-shit old man won't get a job and didn't come home until four this morning." The words overflowed as she brushed a strand of hair from her face. "Sorry. You didn't need to hear all my problems. I'm near my breaking point from the stress."

"Sorry to hear that, ma'am. Sure hope things get better soon."

She nodded and hurried off when someone yelled from the kitchen.

Chuck twisted his mouth, staring out the window again. "When I first came in, I thought she had it made. Pretty face, nice clothes, wedding ring on her finger. Looks can be deceiving."

Similar thoughts ran through Sam's head at first, yet, the recesses of her sleep-deprived eyes suggested otherwise. People often try to hide their pain, but eyes seldom masked the truth. The anger she held toward her husband suggested a projected rudeness toward Chuck.

"Looks like you've had a few bad days yourself." Sam took a sip of coffee. "Want to share your story?"

The rugged-looking fellow stirred his coffee. "Everyone has troubles. No one wants to hear a bunch of whining." He took a sip and set it down.

"I do." Sam met Chuck's stare. "If you're willing to share, of course."

Chuck paused, looking up toward the ceiling. Sam imagined he was trying to decide what to say.

The waitress returned with their platters, placing them gently on the table and offering a half smile. "Here you go, boys. Need anything else?"

"This looks good to me. How about you, Sam?"

"Maybe another cup of coffee, when you get a chance."

"Next time around." She brushed her hands on her apron.

"Thanks."

Steam rose from the fried hash browns. Chuck closed his eyes, drawing in the scent through his nose. "Love potatoes." He folded his hands in prayer and then picked up his fork.

Sam watched with curiosity as Chuck portioned off a section of food on his plate, then began eating from the other side. "My wife, Mutzi, loves potatoes, too. I think she'd eat them at every meal if I cooked them."

"It's the one thing they couldn't destroy in the chow lines."

Sam glanced at Chuck, then picked up his fork. "Army?"

Chuck stopped chewing, squinted his eyes, and Sam's gaze followed Chuck's out the window toward his car. A man walked past the blue sedan and paused, glancing in the front seat. When he moved on, Chuck released a held breath and continued eating.

"Yup. Signed up before they drafted me. Lot of guys hated it, but not me. Finally had a roof over my head and food on the table."

"Rough childhood?"

"You could say that. My dad died before I was born. My mother never recovered from it. Ended up in an orphanage by the time I started school. Let's just say it taught me what I didn't want in life."

The waitress returned and filled their cups, remembering to bring extra cream for Chuck.

"Sure appreciate that, ma'am." He stirred the milk along with some sugar, slow and easy, trying not to spill a drop.

It amazed Sam the things you can learn about people while watching them eat. The man respected and appreciated others, appeared to be spiritual, and showed good table manners. The untouched food on his plate remained a curiosity. Perhaps he was saving some for later.

"How long did you serve?"

"Fifteen years. Best years of my life."

So close to retirement, Sam thought. "Let me guess. Met a woman who didn't want the military life?"

"You got it." Chuck chewed, appearing to savor every bite. He rubbed his stomach which had quieted with the needed meal. "Six months later, she ran off with another man."

Sam shook his head. "Ouch. That hurt."

"Yup. Sure did." Chuck dragged his last bite of toast across half of his plate and stuffed it in his mouth.

"Is that when things started going downhill?"

Silence filled the air. Chuck's eyes hardened. "I wasn't always a street bum."

Regret stuck in Sam's throat. He wished he'd chosen different words, or at least allowed the man to fill in the gap without his prompting. "Didn't mean to suggest you were. Sorry. I was curious what you did when you got out. I retired from the Army a couple years ago and haven't really figured out what I want to do next."

"It's okay. Some bad decisions got me on a path which landed me in a place I shouldn't have been. I paid dearly for my mistakes, but I own them."

The admission reinforced Sam's assessment of the man. Many struggling soldiers failed to accept responsibility for their decisions and actions, often blaming others for their misfortunes.

For the next hour, Chuck shared his painful story. The horrific injustices he'd experienced weighed heavy on Sam's shoulders. There had to be something else he could do to help, but if he helped every homeless guy he'd met, he'd be on the street too.

A quote he'd tried to emulate nagged from the corner of his mind. The late Mother Teresa said, *"Never worry about numbers. Help one person at a time & always start with the person nearest you."*

There *was* something Sam could do. As he listened to the man's unfortunate life tale, Sam formed a plan in his mind, one to help a fellow Army vet regain control of his life.

The waitress returned with one ticket and handed it to Sam. She glanced at Chuck's plate. "Want to take that with you?"

"Yes. Thanks. There's a hungry little fellow waiting in the car."

The waitress gasped. "You left a child in the car?"

Chuck laughed as he shook his head. "I could never do that. He's a four-week old black mutt. The mother left him to make it on his own—kinda like me. Couldn't stand to see it suffer."

The woman placed a hand on her heart. "Wait here. I'll be right back." The waitress hurried off and returned with two bottles of breast milk. "Maybe he'll drink this." She laughed as she handed the bottles to Chuck. "I've got more than enough," she said, gesturing to her swollen chest.

By the time Sam paid the bill, he'd resolved any doubts he might have had about Chuck. He trusted his instincts to see the good in people, and this man had redeeming qualities. He hoped Mutzi would agree. He shook his head, imagining her response to his plan. With a sigh, he whispered to himself, "She'll love the dog, for sure."

Chapter Five

The hike toward the town square did little to sooth Mutzi's frazzled nerves. Marge's sudden interest in their ancestry riled her. "Crap." She clenched her fists into tight balls. "Why dig up the past? Can't change it, but you can sure screw up the future."

She knew Marge believed they were twins. Lots of people doubted it at first, even Mutzi when she was younger, but now they were in their mid-sixties. So what if they didn't look alike, or act alike, or...Mutzi was content with the way things were. If Marge dug deep enough, she'd expose some bones best left covered. Nothing good could come from tilling into their past.

Her stomach knotted tighter as she stepped over each sidewalk crack, a habit she'd formed when superstitions ruled her world. Realizing what she was doing, she came to an abrupt halt. "Damn it," she fussed, again, then scratched the nape of her neck. "Hadn't done that since Sam and I got married."

She folded her arms in defiance, thinking about how life had improved after he'd helped her release the crazy notions dictating her life.

"Ain't going back to that." Mutzi made an about-face and nearly knocked over a woman walking her dog.

"Oh, my!" The blue-haired lady slapped a hand across her chest. "You almost made me fall."

"Sorry." Mutzi bent down and rubbed the ears of the energetic Shih Tzu. "What's her name?"

"Dolly. I named her after Dolly Parton, my favorite singer."

"She's mine, too, because of her Inspiration Library. Did you know she mails free books to children in five different countries? The United States, United Kingdom, Canada, Australia, and the Republic of Ireland."

"Really? I didn't know. Thanks for telling me." The woman tugged on the leash apparently wanting to leave.

Mutzi wasn't quite ready to stop playing with the dog. "Just google her name on the internet."

"Google? Oh, I don't have one of those computer things."

"You can use one at the Lumpkin County Library. Best fact checking place in town." Mutzi stood. "Have a good day, Dolly."

The woman raised a brow. "*We* will. Be sure to watch where you're going so you don't run someone else over."

Mutzi nodded and flipped a hand in the air to wave goodbye as she headed back to Marge's house. Something about animals always changed her spirit. She began singing as she stomped up the steep hill. "The ants go marching one by one..."

Marge rubbed at her neck as she stirred the pot of soup. What would she say to Mutzi when she came back? She didn't mean to upset her by pursuing the ancestry issue, but she wanted—no—needed to confirm her suspicions, even if it meant upsetting her sister.

She walked to the dining room and opened a linen drawer, selecting two of Mutzi's favorite placemats—the ones with kittens on them—and returned to the kitchen island where she prepared the table settings, hoping her sister would cool off and return soon.

The phone call Marge had received the previous week troubled her. What if the caller was right? How would the information effect the family dynamics? As far as Marge was concerned, nothing would change among the three sisters. They'd grown up loving each other and grown stronger when life challenged them. Surely, they wouldn't let whatever she learned in the process of testing her DNA come between them.

The sound of the front door opening interrupted Marge's thoughts. She walked toward the foyer where Mutzi stood. "Hey, Sis. Are you okay?"

Mutzi folded her arms against her chest and nodded. "We need to talk."

"I've got some soup ready in the kitchen. Let's sit in there." Marge removed her apron, disrupting her hair in the process. She paused in front of the hall mirror and smoothed an errant strand.

Mutzi released her folded arms and chuckled. "Wouldn't want one misplaced hair to ruin the day."

Marge smiled. "I miss your little pokes." She glanced in the mirror again. "Guess I've always cared about my looks—maybe a little too much."

"Naw. Just sister-teasing." Mutzi grinned. "You look good. Always have."

Marge stared at her sister, surprised at the quick change in mood. "Thank you. I try." They moved into the kitchen. Marge ladled soup into the bowls and set them on the table. "There's some crackers in the pantry if you want them."

Mutzi closed her eyes and drew in the scent through her nose. "Celery, onions, tomatoes, and melt-in-your-mouth beef—Burgershire Soup—funny name. Who needs crackers when I've got the best soup in town?"

The comment pleased Marge. She'd made a special effort to fix Mutzi's favorites while she was visiting. "Two compliments in one day. Thanks."

Mutzi pulled out a stool and sat down. "You even remembered my favorite placemats. Makes me feel special." She locked eyes with Marge. "Sorry about taking off. Old habits are hard to break."

"I'm sorry I upset you. That wasn't my intention." Marge picked up her napkin. "Do you want to talk about it while we eat?"

Steam rose from the hot bowl of soup. Mutzi gathered a spoonful and blew on it. "I don't understand why you want to do this—now, after all these years."

A knot formed in Marge's stomach. Not sharing the true purpose for her interest bothered Marge, but spreading misinformation disturbed her more. She knew how gossip swelled and she refused to participate in any part of it. For now, Mutzi would have to understand.

"I have reasons I can't share right now. I need to resolve something for myself. When I verify if it's true or not, I promise, I'll share it with you."

Mutzi put the spoon back in her bowl. "You don't trust me?"

"Of course, I do. This is about believing someone else. I need to verify fact from fiction." Marge stared into Mutzi's eyes. "Please, don't worry. Nothing's going to come from this. I promise."

The moment the words left her mouth, Marge regretted them. She knew she had no control over the future or the results of the testing.

Chapter Six

Steady rain accompanied Sam on his return to Dahlonega. The blue sedan kept a safe distance behind him. He'd checked the rearview mirror a hundred times worrying about Chuck's car breaking down in route and making sure not to lose him along the way. The task of explaining his impromptu decision to Mutzi battled for position among his troubled thoughts.

She'd been single and co-dependent on her sister for most of her sixty plus years. Marrying late in life was a challenge for most people. For Mutzi, it required much more, including forgiving Sam for his unexplained disappearance while serving in Vietnam. For years, she'd thought he'd died. A teenage indiscretion shamed her into believing she was responsible, not only for his disappearance, but for her father's untimely death.

She'd become immersed in impractical superstitions which dictated her life. He'd helped her realize they were misconceptions driven by remorse, and she found security in his presence.

Still, they'd been married less than a year. Sam knew it wouldn't be easy for her to accept an outsider into their home, but he believed she'd understand his reasons and consent to the temporary situation.

The headlights following his truck flashed on and off, signaling Chuck needed to make a stop. Sam pulled into a gas station and shut off the motor. Chuck followed, pulling up to a pump. Sam got out of his car and walked toward him.

"I'm riding on fumes." The lanky fellow stuck his hand in his pocket and pulled out a few crumpled dollar bills. "Should have enough to get me there if we don't have too far to go."

"I'll cover this one." Sam withdrew his credit card and stuck it in the slot, punched in some numbers, and returned it to his wallet.

"Not sure why you're doing all this for me." Chuck ran a hand through his unkempt hair.

"Random act of kindness. You'd do the same if you could."

Chuck pressed his lips tight and lowered his eyes. "*I* would, but most people wouldn't."

"I like to think there are still good people in this world willing to help others."

Chuck grunted. "A few. Sure am lucky you're one of them."

"We've got about twenty more miles. Mutzi said one of the college triplets staying with her sister of-fered to give her a ride back to the house about two o'clock. You'll have time to settle in before she arrives."

"I'd like to get cleaned up before she gets there. It's going to be shock enough without finding a bum in her house."

"We'll have a couple hours. No problem." Sam reached into the car and patted the puppy on the back, then rubbed his ears. "Cute little fellow. What's his name?"

"He tags along with me so close I call him Shadow."

"I always believed dogs pick their owners, not the other way around. Guess he adopted you."

Chuck nodded. "I think you're right."

When the gas pump shut off, the two got back in their vehicles and headed toward Dahlonega. Sam turned on the radio, tapping the steering wheel as Willie Nelson sang *On the Road Again*. The last leg of the trip zipped by and soon they were turning onto his property. He grinned as he passed the sign *Welcome to Parks' Place Where Dreams Come True*. He thought about Chuck and wondered if maybe he could help *his* dreams come true. Perhaps.

Sam pulled close to the house and shut off the truck's motor. He closed his eyes and stretched his legs before getting out, tired from the confined position and glad to be back home.

As he reached for the handle, Chuck pulled the door open and offered a hand to help him out. Sam pivoted and stood. His knee buckled and Chuck grabbed his arm to steady him.

"Watch it there, friend. Don't want you to break something."

"Thanks. I have to get used to my new leg. Takes a bit for it to cooperate."

Chuck glanced around, taking in the acres of peacefulness. "You've got a little piece of Heaven here." His eyes met Sam's. "Sure your old lady's gonna like you bringing a beat up relic home?" He hung his head. "I'd sure hate to come home and find me here."

"Mutzi's a fine woman. It might take her a little while to adjust, but she'll come around. Treat her with respect and she'll do the same." Sam held onto the bed of the truck and pulled out his bag. "Let's get you settled in. After a shower and shave, you'll feel better about yourself."

"That couldn't hurt." He reached through the open window of his car, took out a handful of clothes, a near-empty pack of cigarettes, and Shadow. He set the dog down on the ground and it stayed glued to Chuck's leg. "Is it okay to bring him in while I clean up? I'll keep him locked in the bedroom. He doesn't bark and I've been training him to not make a mess."

Sam nodded. "That's fine, for now."

Chuck hesitated and looked around as if trying to find something. "I think maybe we should wait a day or two for your wife to adjust to me being here before telling her about Shadow."

"I think she'll be thrilled."

Chuck shook his head. "I'd rather wait, if that's possible."

"If you insist." Sam shrugged and pointed to the back of the house. "The previous owners left a dog-house out back behind the shed. Mutzi seldom goes out there. I seem to remember a leash, too." He tipped his head and stared at Chuck. "You sure about this? I'm telling you. Mutzi loves animals."

"I think it'd be better to wait a few days. By the way, I could use a washing machine, too, if it's not too much trouble."

"No trouble at all. I forgot to mention. There's no smoking in the house."

"Been needing to quit. No time like the present." He tossed the pack of Marlboro's back into his car.

Chapter Seven

Mutzi hung on tight as Brandi maneuvered the purple Vespa over winding hills and around tight curves like a pro. The heart-thumping experience proved to be exactly what Mutzi needed to release the tension which built worrying about her sister's newest quest.

Marge's protest about Mutzi's mode of transportation still echoed in her mind. "You are not riding on the back of that thing!" You'd think by now Marge would know her sister well enough to know she couldn't tell her not to do something. It only made her want to do it more.

No matter how Marge had tried, she'd not been successful in changing the quirky, eccentric ways Mutzi lived her life. Not a piece of clothing in Mutzi's wardrobe came close to Marge's trendy, sophisticated style. Bold colors, cheerful animal prints, and outrageous patterns brought Mutzi joy and she didn't care what others thought about it.

Last year Mutzi had nearly sent Marge over the edge worrying about the faux gold bricks she created for the Gold Rush Festival, an annual event celebrating Dahlonega being the first gold rush town in the

United States. The bricks turned out to be the biggest money maker for the Dahlonega Woman's Club. Marge fussed about storing apples and potatoes in the gold bricks for a week or more. Much like the warning about the Vespa, it fell on deaf ears and turned out well.

Despite the noise and being buffeted by the wind, the ride proved to be exhilarating. She watched Clyde Jones wag his finger at them as they sped past PJ's Rusted Buffalo leather store in the town square and turned onto the road leading to Sam's place. Mutzi doubted the ancient guy had time to recognize her with the helmet on, but she wished he had. Sometimes she enjoyed feeding the gossip mill.

Traffic slowed as they neared a busy intersection. Mutzi called out to Brandi, "Turn left here. About a mile down this road, you'll make a sharp right."

Once they turned off the main highway, Brandi slowed around the narrow curves and over the next couple of hills. Mutzi tapped her shoulder and pointed a finger toward their ranch house. "Cross over the creek bridge." As they crossed it, she pointed to the sign she'd given Sam for Christmas last year.

Brandi gave her a thumbs up.

An unfamiliar blue sedan with rusted fenders was parked behind Sam's truck, catching Mutzi's attention as they rode up the blacktop drive. When they came to a stop, she swung a leg over the seat and hopped off, removing her helmet. "Don't recognize that heap. Wonder who's here."

Brandi removed her helmet and ran a hand through her cropped carrot top. "Georgia plates. Must be a local."

By the time they reached the porch, Sam opened the door and stepped out.

"How's my favorite girl?" He wrapped his arms around Mutzi and tried to kiss her.

Mutzi gave him a peck on the cheek and stretched her neck to the side searching for the owner of the car. "Who's here?"

A lanky fellow, with damp hair in need of cut, sauntered onto the porch. "The name's Chuck. Nice to meet you, ma'am." He stuck out his calloused hand waiting for Mutzi to respond.

Mutzi stood firm and studied his face. She hadn't seen him before, but there was something about him that didn't sit right in her mind. She shot a glare at Sam. "What's he doing here?"

Sam avoided her question by diverting his attention to Brandi. "Good to see you. I really appreciate you bringing Mutzi home."

The young woman shrugged. "No problem. I was heading across town anyway. She directed her attention toward Chuck. "Brandi. Brandi McDougal."

"Nice to meet you. Sam tells me you and your sisters are staying at Marge's while attending college."

"Yup. Last week of the semester."

Chuck walked down the stairs and stood next to the Vespa. "Nice wheels. Always wanted to ride on one of those things."

"Come on. I'll give you a ride." Brandi attempted to take the helmet from Mutzi.

Mutzi gripped it tight. "You don't know this man or anything about him."

Brandi shrugged. "It's just a ride. Pretty harmless since I'm the one driving."

"Girl, you've got a lot to learn. You can't trust *anybody* these days." Mutzi glared at Chuck.

Brandi yanked the helmet from Mutzi and tossed it to Chuck. "YOLO."

Mutzi's face burned as she watched the two speed off. "What the hell does that mean?"

"You only live once." Sam put an arm around Mutzi. "She'll be fine. Come on inside. We've got some catching up to do."

Chapter Eight

Where are we going?" Chuck yelled into the wind as Brandi maneuvered the motor scooter into a parking lot.

She pulled near the entrance and shut off the Vespa. "They're hiring for the summer. Need money to pay for my new wheels." The red-head whipped off her helmet, tucked it under her arm, and headed for the front door of the Consolidated Gold Mine.

Chuck got off the bike. "Wait up. I'm going to need a job, too." This fast-moving girl intrigued him. Unpredictable. Full of energy. Unrestricted. She also concerned him. He'd known a young woman much like her. She'd managed to get into deep trouble, and he'd paid a severe price for her friendship. Still, he was at her mercy for the time being since he had no other transportation back to Sam's.

The notion of working at a gold mine interested Chuck. He'd read enticing stories of men panning for gold, but never dreamed he'd have a chance to try it. There were worse places to work, and you never know, a nice chunk of gold could sure make a difference in his lifestyle. He hurried to catch up with Brandi.

A young man wearing a snug t-shirt that emphasized his muscled arms, released a slow growl as Brandi walked through the door. He reached out and took her hands as if they were old friends. "And what brings a fine lassie like you here today?"

Her eyes glistened as the man spoke, apparently smitten by his attention. "Two o'clock interview. I'm running a few minutes late."

A smirk swathed the guy's face as he extended a hand and directed her through a side door. Chuck's stomach turned. Too cocky. Full of himself. This guy spelled trouble. He sensed it in his bones.

As Chuck roamed the gift shop, the number of customers milling around amazed him. Thousands of souvenirs filled the display tables, attracting the attention of squealing children. Everything in the spacious room glittered. He stopped at a display case where small treasure boxes held sealed vials of gold slivers. Lifting one of the tiny bottles from a purple, velvet-lined box, he watched minuscule flakes flicker as they floated in the water. Fool's gold? He wondered how one could tell the difference.

Across the room, a man and woman sat near a glass partition. On the other side of it, a bright light shined over the shoulder of an older gentleman who wore strange eye glasses with magnifiers on both lenses as he etched lettering onto a gold band. A sign next to them read *Custom made jewelry*.

Chuck tried to imagine ever having enough money to custom order anything, much less a ring. Even before losing his job when the animal shelter had to close, he struggled to scratch enough money to keep food on the table and heat the small motel room he rented. No longer able to even afford the luxury of a room, his aging car had served as shelter for the past three months.

The energetic red-head punched him in the arm. "We start Monday."

The exuberant voice startled Chuck, causing him to stumble. He reached out to grab the closest thing in sight, a tall glass jewelry display case, and it shifted. Brandi rushed to steady it before it tipped over.

"Close one, Chuck." She motioned toward the door. "We better get out of here now, or we'll lose our jobs before we even start."

She grabbed his hand and pulled him toward the exit.

When they reached the door, Chuck broke free from her grip and stopped, trying to make sense of her words. "What do you mean *we?*"

"I told the guy who hired me, Domenic something or other, I'd only come to work for him if you could too."

"But you don't know anything about me. You don't even know my full name."

"You said you needed a job, right? And you must be a friend of Sam, who is a great guy, so that means you must be pretty great yourself." Brandi snapped her helmet in place and threw a leg over the scooter. "Time's a wasting. Let's go."

Chuck shook his head, stunned at the naivety of the brassy young woman. "You've got a lot to learn, girl."

The bike helmet added to the pressure building in Chuck's skull as they zoomed down the winding road back to Sam's place. How could a guy hire someone he'd never even spoken to? What was in it for him? Was he so desperate for help and if so, why?

Years of experience with criminals made him wary of bold moves by unscrupulous men. What would he expect from this girl in return?

As for Chuck, he could handle most anything, as long as it was legit. It didn't matter what the hours were or how much he made. He needed work, for as long as he could get it. For as long as his past...stayed in the past.

Chapter Nine

As Marge shook excess rain from her umbrella and opened her front door, the house phone started ringing. She hurried inside and lifted the receiver, catching the call before it went to the recorder. "Hello."

"Ciao."

"Rose Ellen?" Marge slipped the damp cashmere pashmina off her shoulders and hung it on the coat rack as she juggled the phone with her other hand.

"That's me. Oh, the connection's so much clearer on your house phone. I could hardly understand you last time I called on the cell."

"It's good to hear your voice, too. How are you?"

"Stupendo. We're sitting on a bella veranda sipping caffé." Her voice faded for a moment. "Was that right, Roberto?"

Her older sister's strained effort to speak Italian made Marge grin. Age would never stop Rose Ellen from learning a new language. Ever since she'd returned to Dahlonega last year and sold her New York boutique, Marge had watched her blossom.

Meeting Roberto seemed to be exactly what Rose Ellen needed, someone who treated her as his equal, and lavished her with the attention of a queen. He'd also fulfilled her longing to travel abroad.

"Si, my dear. Splendido." The baritone voice echoed in the background. "Ciao, Marge."

"Greetings, Roberto."

Rose Ellen giggled. "He still gives me goosebumps when he talks."

Marge smiled to herself. "He's quite the charmer. I'm so happy you found each other."

"How are things there? Is Mutzi behaving herself?"

Marge paused, remembering her twin speeding off behind Brandi, ignoring the warnings she shouted. "Things are fine. Mutzi visited for a few days while Sam was in the hospital having his prosthesis replaced. In fact, she left a little while ago, on some kind of motorcycle, mind you."

"She bought a motorcycle?'

"No. No. Brandi gave her a ride on the back of a ...Vespa, I think they call it."

"I bet she was a sight to see. They have those everywhere in Italy. Maybe I'll make Roberto take me for a ride on one while we're here." Rose Ellen laughed. "Good for Mutzi. She still has a lot of spunk at her age."

"Spunk. Well, that's not what I'd call it, but we'll go with that for now."

"Roberto's been taking me to meet all his relatives. He has such an interesting heritage, it makes me wish I knew more about ours."

The statement surprised Marge and provided an opportunity to tell her about the DNA test. "Do you really?"

"I do. You never know, we may be related to some important person."

"Well, I'm not looking for fame, but...I did something that might surprise you. I ordered a kit to test my DNA, and I'm thinking about taking an ancestry course at the library." She paused, waiting for Rose Ellen's response, remembering Mutzi's earlier distressed reaction.

"Really? How exciting. I should get mine tested, too." Rose Ellen's voice trailed off, apparently telling Roberto about our conversation. "It's so funny that we both were thinking the same thing."

"Mutzi didn't think it was funny. In fact, she was quite upset. She doesn't want anything to do with it."

"Oh, don't let her discourage you. She'll get over it." Rose Ellen took a quick breath and continued. "When we get the results, we can plan a trip to whatever countries our relatives are from. Wouldn't that be exciting?"

"Sounds like a perfect opportunity for you...and Roberto. You both love to travel. I'm content to stay in

Georgia, and you know Mutzi would never get on a plane." The idea of leaving the US made Marge's pulse quicken and not in a good way. Busy airports, foreign languages, exchanging currency. No thanks. She'd stay put in the south.

"You're probably right. We'll talk about it when I get back."

"When are you coming home?"

"May 1st, just in time for my birthday. I'll be seventy. I told Roberto my sisters would be planning a big party." She paused. "You are...right?"

Marge's hand flew to cover her mouth. She'd nearly forgotten. "Of course. We'll do something very special." Marge hurried into the study and grabbed a pen and paper, making a note.

"By the way, what made you decide to get into the ancestry thing?"

"I—um..." Marge didn't want to lie, but she wasn't ready to discuss the true reason. Not yet. She glanced up at her late husband's photo, looking for help in forming her response. Almost as if he obliged, static on the phone made it difficult to hear.

"Oh, for goodness sakes. That noise is terrible. I can't stand it. I'll call again later." As Rose Ellen shouted "Ciao" the phone went dead.

Chapter Ten

The afternoon sun faded behind the towering oaks. Mutzi pulled the knee-length cable knit sweater snug around her waist as she climbed the mountainous hill that overlooked Sam's place.

Sam's place. Mutzi still resisted calling it her place, even though Sam reminded her of it often. Perhaps it was a remnant from living under Marge's roof for so many years. Still, day's like today didn't help. Her husband, the man she loved, the man she thought she knew well, had invited a stranger to come live with them...without even asking her. How was she supposed to accept that decision without feeling resentment?

She'd listened to his reasoning. Chuck, a former vet, was homeless, living in his car. He needed a helping hand. That was good enough for Sam. His heart, bigger than all of Georgia, couldn't stand to walk away knowing he could have done more than offering a hot meal.

It wasn't as easy for Mutzi. Having a stranger in their home made her anxious. It meant change, something that always challenged her. It had taken a year for her to become comfortable with being married and living away from her sister's protective hand. Now, the ground shifted, leaving her balance unstable. She'd decided to walk and think, rather than storm out like she had at Marge's house.

Sam did everything to comfort and reassure her. She appreciated it. And she knew her love for Sam included his kind heart. Still, having another man under foot every day troubled her. What did they know about him? Was he a freeloader looking for an easy target? Was he dangerous? She'd been fooled before and paid the price. By the time Mutzi reached the top of the hill, she knew what she needed to do. She turned around and headed back to the house.

She heard the whine of the Vespa in the distance and watched the two riders weave to the left and right in unified motion as they hugged each curve. By the time they drove up the drive, she'd walked onto the porch. The two greeted her, their cheeks rosy from being windblown and chilled by the crisp spring day.

Brandi high-fived Mutzi. "Got the job."

"That's great. When do you start?"

Brandi nodded toward Chuck. "*We* start training on Monday."

Mutzi frowned. "Say what?"

"I worked a deal and got us both a job." She took the helmet from Chuck and strapped it to the scooter. "I think Chuck's still in shock."

Chuck shook his head. "I am. All I said was I needed a job, too. She did the rest." He reached out a hand toward Brandi. "Much obliged."

"They must have been desperate for help." The words flew out of Mutzi's mouth before she could bite them back. Part of her regretted it, but until she knew more about this man, she'd have a hard time being civil to him.

Brandi's mouth opened. She glanced toward Chuck who had turned away. Pressing her lips tight, she donned her helmet, and hopped onto the scooter. "Gotta run. Nice meeting you, Chuck. See you Monday." Her eyes met Mutzi's. "You need to chill. Give the guy a break."

Sam walked onto the porch as Brandi zoomed away. "Guess you can scratch 'riding a Vespa' off your bucket list."

Chuck nodded. "I got more than a ride from her." He tugged at his flannel shirt, tucking the tattered tail into his clean, weathered jeans.

Sam's eyes widened. "What do you mean?"

"That girl's something else. Somehow she got me hired, too." He cupped his hand around his chin, rubbing his clean-shaven face. "She's in for some rude awakenings. Someone needs to keep an eye on her."

Mutzi glared at Sam, mentally sending him a message. *That someone better not be Chuck.* She hoped he wasn't some kind of pervert. The man was old enough to be the girl's grandfather.

Sam shrugged his shoulders as if to say he had no control over the matter. He held open the door. "Dinner's ready." When no one moved, Sam sauntered back inside.

Chuck extended a hand motioning for Mutzi to go first.

Something about the man, something unexplainable rattled her. She locked eyes with him. "Don't know who you are, or what your story is"—she pointed two fingers at her eyes and then toward him—"but I'm watching you." Stomping up the steps, she paused at the door with one more warning. "And stay away from Brandi. She's just a kid."

"Yes, ma'am."

She knew what she needed to do. When they finished eating, she'd take things into her own hands.

Chapter Eleven

As dawn filtered through the plantation blinds, Mutzi eased out of bed, silent as a preying cat, slipped on a robe, and tiptoed down the hall toward the kitchen. The unwelcomed stranger in her house gnawed away at her all night, making sleep come in spurts between unsettling nightmares.

The aroma of brewed coffee filled her senses. "Damn it." She yanked at the opening of the bunny-covered flannel robe and pulled it snug around her neck. With Sam still sleeping, she knew Chuck must already be up. "Just like him to ruin my plans."

For two days she'd tried to find time to herself, but between Sam and Chuck, someone was always around. "Damn it," she muttered again. This arrangement wasn't going to work.

She filled her mug with the steamy beverage and peeked out the door onto the porch. "Crap." Her voice was loud enough to draw Chuck's attention. "Even got my favorite spot." She glared at him, wishing him away.

He jumped up, fumbling the empty cup he cradled in his hand, but catching it before it crashed to the floor. "Morning, missus." He stepped away from the swing and moved toward the stairs, extending a hand toward the seat.

Mutzi offered a grunt and turned away, looking out over the dew-covered acreage. *Why am I being such a bitch to this man?* So far he'd been polite and considerate to her. Hadn't left a mess in the bathroom or kitchen. He listened to all their crazy anecdotes without interrupting, laughed at her silly jokes while they sat around the campfire, and even entertained them by playing the harmonica—pretty well, too.

Unexplained little things seemed to irritate her about him. Like the way he'd disappear every so often without saying where he was going. She thought maybe he was sneaking a smoke or worse, a joint, when he was out of their sight, but she hadn't smelled anything to support her suspicions.

It drove her crazy that he snuck food from the fridge when they weren't looking, not because he couldn't have whatever he wanted, but because he did it on the sly.

The thing concerning Mutzi the most still weighed on her mind. His past. Whenever she asked questions, he seemed to find a way to avoid answering them. Didn't help when Sam kept changing the subject. Not knowing more about him frustrated her. The man hid something, she felt it in her bones.

Sam suggested Chuck's homelessness might be the reason she didn't trust him. Hell, if it weren't for Marge, it could have happened to Mutzi more than once over the years. She knew the answer, the real problem, but didn't want to admit it. Regardless, she found it disrupting having him underfoot.

It wasn't her nature to be judgmental. She disliked people who did that. Deciding to give it another shot, she turned back toward Chuck. "Want some breakfast?"

The corner of his mouth inched a little higher. "Thanks, but I don't want to be a bother."

Mutzi let out a sigh. "Ya look like you're gonna float away with the next gust of wind. Come on in. I'll scramble up something, but don't expect much. Sam does most of the cooking around here." She stopped and looked at him. "Bet you've never burnt down a kitchen before." She snickered as she drew open the door, letting Chuck through first.

Chuck's face lit with a broad smile. "Can't say as I have ma'am."

As Mutzi pulled out a cast iron skillet, preparing to get started, Sam strolled into the kitchen.

"Good morning. You two got an early start on me. Didn't hear either of you get up." Sam walked to Mutzi and gave her a kiss.

She noticed his fresh shave, pressed trousers and dress shirt. Drawing her brows tight, she worried. "Where you going?" Surely, he wouldn't expect her to entertain his guest all day.

Sam picked up an empty mug and filled it with coffee. "Reverend Mitch invited me to help plan the Easter services. Remember? We're meeting with the parish council this morning." He set his drink down on the countertop and took the skillet from Mutzi. "I should be back by noon."

She held onto the handle and met Sam's eyes. "Is Chuck going with you?"

Sam glanced at Chuck. "You're welcome to come along."

He shook his head. "I'm going to drive around town and get familiar with the layout, check out the library and see if I can remember how to get back to the gold mine."

Mutzi released the pan along with some building tension. Having the house to herself was just what she wanted...no needed. With both men gone, she'd have time to do the research she hadn't gotten a chance to do.

"How many eggs this morning?" Sam turned on the burner and slapped a spoonful of butter into the skillet.

Chuck paused, looking from Mutzi to Sam. Finally, he responded, "Three would be great, if you have enough for everyone."

"No problem. Got a couple dozen in the fridge. Three it is. How about you, Mutzi?"

Mutzi pulled a carton and a large ham steak from the refrigerator. She handed the meat to Sam, setting the eggs to the side of the counter next to the stove. "Two, scrambled. I'll put some toast on."

Chuck moved to the sink and washed his hands. "I'll set the table, if that's okay? What plates do you want to use?"

Mutzi pointed to the left while opening a drawer near the sink. "Napkins are in the cupboard."

Within fifteen minutes, the three of them sat at a table full of food.

Mutzi waited for Sam to begin his morning blessing before the meal. She extended her hand to him. Chuck extended one toward Sam and the other toward her. She hesitated, then accepted the rough, sturdy hand.

Sam began, "Lord, you've brought the three of us together for a purpose. With your guidance, may we fulfill your trust in us to provide for others whenever we have the opportunity. Help us to be accepting of one another and to make each day better...especially, for those most in need." His eyes lifted for a moment, then closed again. "Bless this food we are about to share. Amen."

Mutzi and Chuck responded "Amen" in harmony. She squirmed in her chair knowing the message was meant more for her than anyone else. It'd take great effort, but she vowed in her heart to try to be kinder to Chuck.

Chapter Twelve

Mutzi slid her finger between the wooden slats of the kitchen blinds and peeked out the window watching Chuck drive away in his aging rattletrap. As he rounded the corner and faded from sight, she shuffled down the hall into her "babe cave" to get her investigation underway.

A sense of peace filled her spirit as she moved through the special sanctuary. It happened every time she entered the room. Her beloved books filled the orange, yellow, and blue cubes secured to the wall. She brushed her hand over the spine of *The Lion, The Witch, and the Wardrobe* and then *All Creatures Great and Small*. They spoke to her in quiet whispers, each having reflective meaning and purpose, much like every corner of the special retreat Sam had created for her.

She wandered toward the large bay window overlooking a meadow of red ruffle azaleas and lush green shrubs. She opened the window and drew in the sweet fragrance of the deciduous plants. Birds danced through the shadows of the bushes singing delightful tunes that matched the joy filling Mutzi's heart.

A bright pink pillow rested on the snow-white hammock Sam had suspended from the ceiling in the room, and she couldn't resist stroking its plush fabric as she thought about the time and effort Sam had devoted to designing the space for her. It was more than an escape haven, used when anxieties overwhelmed her, it also served as a continuous reminder of the depth of Sam's loving and ever-giving heart.

She stepped closer to the antique roll-top desk, opened the laptop, and brought the machine to life. Still standing, she cupped a curled hand to her mouth, not quite ready to commit to what seemed so clear last night. A pang of guilt washed over her as she settled her eyes on the screen. Torn between trusting Sam's judgement and her deep-seated fear of strangers, she hesitated.

Who was she to question Sam's decision to invite a stranger into their home? Digging into Chuck's background felt like a betrayal of Sam. How would he react if he found out? She knew it wouldn't matter to Sam what Chuck had done in the past.

Trust came easy for him.

Not for Mutzi.

Her reason, buried deep in the recesses of her soul, formed the person she was today. The intense physical pain that penetrated her body that night—the night she still refused to speak of fifty years later—

wasn't nearly as agonizing as the emotional disappointment in personally learning there was evil in her world. Evil so despicable it shattered her innocence and crushed her essence, leaving a broken and sometimes bitter creature in its place.

Mutzi pulled the chair away from the oak desk and eased onto it. She stared at the screen, struggling with her decision. What if she didn't check and he turned out to be evil? She feared for Brandi. Chuck could be a serial killer or rapist. He and Brandi would be working together starting next week. She'd never forgive herself if something happened to that child, something terrible...something that could have been prevented. If only she'd been warned.

Her shaky fingers found the keyboard and began to move with urgency. Within a few minutes, she realized the fruitlessness of her search. There were hundreds of men with his name. She berated herself for not finding out his middle name or from where he'd been born.

She tried to estimate the year of his birth, thinking they were close to the same age. His license plates indicated he lived in Georgia, which helped reduce the number of options. Still, with the thousand possibilities, she failed to learn anything about the stranger.

"I'm back."

The unexpected voice made Mutzi jump to her feet, spinning toward the door, unaware her foot was tangled in the electric cord. The tug sent her laptop flying off the desk.

Chuck rushed into the room, snagging his shoe on a throw rug, and sending him lunging toward her with outspread arms. The sudden flailing motion triggered a horrific memory. His jagged fingernail scraped down her arm, drawing a trail of blood. No longer present in the moment, Mutzi screamed, her voice echoing through the once silent room and out the open window.

Chuck rolled onto his back and groaned as he grabbed his right knee. "I'm sorry. I'm so sorry."

The red fluid oozing from Mutzi's wound sent her over the edge. "Get out!"

Chuck rolled over and scrambled to his feet, his eyes wide with confusion.

"Get out!" The words spit from Mutzi's mouth so hard and fast, Chuck ducked as if she'd thrown something at him.

"Yes, ma'am. I'll pack my things." He turned to leave. "I'm sorry."

Mutzi bent down, picked up the laptop and placed it on the desk. She lowered herself into the desk chair and reached for a tissue.

Sam rushed into the room. "What's going on in here? I could hear you clear down the road."

She didn't answer, still shaken from the awkward mishap.

Sam noticed the drips of blood on the hardwood floor and his eyes traveled up to Mutzi's arm. "What in the world happened?"

Mutzi stood and tried to get past Sam. "I need to clean this up."

He took hold of her arm "I'll take care of it. Tell me what happened. How did you get cut?"

She jerked away. "Damn fool scared the shit out of me." She rushed across the hall into their bedroom and slammed the door behind her.

Chapter Thirteen

Despite the closed door, Sam followed her into the bedroom. Mutzi sat on the edge of the bed and watched him wet a cloth in the bathroom and bring it to her. With the tenderness he always showed, he gently wiped the traces of blood from her forearm.

"Talk to me. You don't usually scream when someone startles you, and you certainly don't end up a bloody mess." He placed a finger under her chin and lifted it, staring into her eyes. "Something else is going on."

The horrific memory, buried for years, choked her throat. She pushed it back down again, unwilling to release it. Mutzi swallowed hard and looked away, not wanting Sam to see the tears threatening to spill. "I—I'm having trouble with him being here."

Sam stood and took Mutzi's hands in his. "Did he do something to you?" He held up her arm. "Did he do this?"

She shook her head. Chuck wasn't the problem and she regretted her words. "No. Yes, His nail caught my arm when I swung at him." She took the damp cloth from Sam and pressed it against the wound.

"Swung at him?"

"He lunged at me—when he tripped—trying to catch the laptop." Her head dropped and she closed her eyes. "Doesn't matter. It wasn't his fault."

Sam sat back down. "What is it then? What's bothering you?"

An uncooperative tear slid down her cheek and she brushed it away. "I don't want to talk about it. Not now."

"All right. But when you're ready, we need to discuss it. I need to know what's going on in that busy little head of yours." He half-grinned, revealing one of his delightful dimples.

"Guess I better go check on Chuck. I think he hurt himself when he fell." She stood and dropped a peck on Sam's lips. "I probably scared the shit out of him, too."

"Want me to come with you?"

Mutzi shook her head. "Naw. My mess to clean up, not yours." She eased down the hall to the extra bedroom where she'd first stayed when she moved in with Sam. It seemed like a lifetime ago in some ways, and yet, in others, it was fresh in her mind.

The decision to live with him before they married hadn't been easy. Though she loved Sam intensely, there were things she'd never told him. Things she'd never told anyone. Things she'd kept silenced until today. Somehow, Sam sensed her need to feel safe and had done everything he could to make it happen.

The periwinkle walls remained untouched, as did the stars that covered the ceiling, and the green paisley bedspread. Sam put so much effort into making the space feel like home for her, and it served its purpose well. Now, it should have been a safe haven for someone else, had she not gone bonkers and scared him to death.

She watched as Chuck placed a rolled-up flannel shirt into a plastic bag that served as his suitcase. When he turned to pick up the yellow and pink pillows he'd placed on the dresser, he realized she was standing there.

"I'm almost done. I'll be out in a few minutes."

Mutzi walked toward him and took the pillows, placing them on the rocker in the corner of the room. "No. You should stay." Her eyes met his. "I'm—sorry."

"Ma'am, I didn't mean to scare you."

"I know that." She drew in a deep breath and released it. "You got the brunt of something you weren't responsible for. I'm sorry."

"Not the first time, ma'am." He paused and took a breath. "There's a few things I need to tell you."

She studied his face, sensing an unexplained comradery. "Think we both need to air a few things.

It's time we talk turkey. There's a bench under a nice shade tree. Can your knee handle a walk out back?"

Chuck flinched. "Sure. But, I better tell you one thing before we go out there." He cleared his throat. "I brought a buddy with me. Been hiding him hoping you'd get used to me before I introduced you to him."

Mutzi jerked back. "A...buddy?"

Chuck smiled. "A four-legged one...his name's Shadow."

"A dog? You've been hiding a dog from ME?" Now it all made sense. Food vanishing from the fridge. Chuck disappearing for what she thought were smoke breaks. Even the whining Sam attributed to a neighbor's mutt.

With a playful punch to Chuck's arm, Mutzi shook her head. "You two did this all wrong. Should have introduced the mutt first, and then eased *you* in later." The laugh that roared from her belly felt good. "Let's go rescue the poor guy."

The two headed out the back door toward the shed, far in the corner of their large yard. The small black lab jumped up and down as they approached. Mutzi bent, unhooked the leash, and picked up the bundle of fur. The excited animal licked her face and leapt in her arms, seeming to ignore Chuck in the background.

"I see how this is going to be. I rescue you and then when someone else comes along, you discard me like a worn out shoe." He chuckled as he rubbed the dog's ear.

"Shadow, huh? He's pretty darn cute."

"Yeah. The way he clung to me after his mother stopped feeding him made it seem appropriate."

Mutzi nodded toward the bench. "Don't forget we got some talking to do."

Chuck nodded. "I haven't forgotten."

They sat and the dog jumped from one lap to the other, eager for attention from both of them. "Why don't you start by telling me where you're from?"

"Not much to tell. Grew up outside Gainesville. My father died before I was born. Mother never got over it." He released a heavy sigh. "She passed when I was five. From there I spent years bouncing back and forth from an orphanage to foster families. Decided I'd run away when I was sixteen. Lived on the streets for a while, then enlisted when I was old enough."

Mutzi listened as she fiddled with Shadow. "Rough start."

"Got better when I joined the Army. At least I had food and a purpose. Probably saved my life."

She rocked back and forth as she held the comforting animal, appreciating the simple life she enjoyed as a child. It wasn't easy without a mother, but she couldn't imagine losing both parents.

"Like a fool, I got out a few years before I could have retired. Planned to marry and start a family." He covered his mouth with his weathered hand as he reminisced.

"Guessing that didn't work out?"

"Nope. She had other plans." He massaged his knee. "Got a job in construction. Worked as many hours as I could to keep my mind off things. Didn't help much, but I built up a fine bank account." He shook his head. "Got scammed out of all my savings by someone who claimed to be a friend. Ended up living in a rundown motel..."

Mutzi watched as the color drained from the man's face. As tough as his life had been, she anticipated it got worse. His distant stare suggested a heavy weight burdening his soul. A burden he didn't dare to share with many. She gave him a few minutes of quiet reflection.

"Your story's safe with me."

He cleared his throat and looked into her eyes. "I went to prison—for murder."

There it was. The admission rattled around in her head, but she forced herself not to overreact. Instead, she handed him the puppy and turned toward him to listen with her heart.

Chapter Fourteen

Marge dried the heavy aluminum cookie sheet and bent to slip it into the bottom drawer of the stove. When she stood, she was startled to see Chelsea standing in the doorway watching her. "Oh, goodness. I thought you left with your sisters."

"I'm sorry. I didn't mean to scare you." Chelsea wrapped a finger around a strand of her red hair and twirled it. "I did leave with them. They don't know I came back."

Marge patted her hand on one of the bar stools, motioning to the young woman to sit. "Is everything all right?"

"Yes...well...sort of." With her elbows on the island, Chelsea folded her hands and pressed them to her chin.

Clearly, something bothered the girl and Marge wanted to give her time to express it. "I'll put on a pot of water for tea." Removing two mugs from the cabinet, Marge set them on the counter and opened the apothecary jar. "Shall we try lemongrass?"

"Sounds good. Thanks." Chelsea released a sigh. "My professors let me take my finals early."

Marge eased onto one of the stools. "That seems a little unusual. Are you going somewhere?"

Chelsea drew in a deep breath and let it out slowly. "I applied for an art internship and got it. I'll be a docent and shadowing a staff member of an art museum."

The news surprised Marge. She knew the girl had special talents and wanted to pursue a career in art. "How exciting. Congratulations. Which museum?"

"The British Museum." Chelsea's eyes met Marge's.

The name slowly registered with Marge. "In England? Oh, goodness." For a brief moment, Marge tried to imagine traveling to another country at such a young age. The thought unsettled her, but she knew it was the chance of a lifetime for Ashley. "What a prestigious opportunity. I bet your sisters are extremely proud of you."

Chelsea lowered her eyes. "I haven't told them." She twirled a strand of hair, pulling it across her flush cheek. "I told my parents and they thought it was great. My sisters will be upset. We've never been apart. I have to tell them soon, but I don't want them to be mad at me."

The kettle whistled on the stove and Marge stood to turn off the burner. She turned and walked around the island and took Chelsea's hands in hers. "I think I understand. I remember when Mutzi and I were your age. I earned a full ride for a college in Atlanta. Being away from my twin for the first time wasn't easy, of course. But, we survived, and so will the three of you."

"We all agreed to go to the same college and insisted on staying in the same dorm. That's how we ended up here with you. I feel like I'm abandoning them."

"It's part of becoming adults, honey. It's not like you're leaving them forever. Your sister-bond will always be strong." Marge gave Chelsea a hug. "It's going to be okay." She held her for a moment and then said, "Whenever our family has something heavy to discuss, we have a family dinner. How about we do that with your sisters tonight?"

A smile lifted the frown from Chelsea's face. "Okay." She leaned in and gave Marge a tender kiss on her cheek. "Thank you...for being you. Your wisdom has been a blessing to all of us."

The words filled Marge's heart with joy. "You're very welcome."

Chapter Fifteen

Chuck pulled into the empty parking lot of Consolidated Gold Mine and shut off the engine. Often his punctuality resulted in waiting on something or someone else, but it was a life-long habit.

As he glanced around, the mixed message of the landscaping confused him. Obviously a great deal of time and money had been spent creating what was once an attractive garden, but the unattractive weeds and serious lack of water screamed neglect.

A sleek black car screeched to a halt in a space near the door. Chuck recognized the car's logo from mythology—a trident—designed after the pitch-fork like image Neptune carried.

The man opened the driver's door of the Maserati and stepped out, flicking a cigarette into a patch of pansies in desperate need of water.

Chuck shook his head and muttered, "Unbelievable." In the thirty seconds that had passed, Chuck had confirmed the gut feeling he had about the man who'd hired him and Brandi. No respect.

Anyone who'd smoke inside an exquisite Italian car and then flick a lit cigarette into a drought-stricken patch of anything, inches away from his car and business, probably lived off someone else's money.

Chuck had considered waiting for Brandi to arrive before going in, but he needed to introduce himself and establish what he could offer the business. Tagging onto someone else's coattails didn't reflect his personality. After spending time at the library researching the connection of the gold mine to the history of the town, he'd prepared a list of his skills and knowledge that were adaptable to the work he might perform.

He'd vowed to himself, no matter what, he'd do his best to keep this job, grateful for the unexpected opportunity. As he walked toward the entrance, a whisper edged forth from the shadows of his mind. *Until my past resurfaces.* He drew in a deep breath, tucked it back into place, and marched forward through the hefty wooden door.

Mr. Maserati flipped wall switches and the large entrance filled with light, revealing a fine layer of dust on the display case. He turned and stared at Chuck, his thick near-black brows drawn together. "Who are you?"

Chuck stepped forward and extended his hand. "Milford—Charles Hansen. Call me Chuck."

Ignoring the offer, the man's eyes traveled up and down, taking in Chuck's worn, but clean, attire.

"You hired me last week, along with a young woman."

His brows tightened, creating a crease along his forehead. As he seemed to remember, a smirk made his left cheek rise. "Ah, yes. Mandi something or other."

"Brandi McDougal," Chuck corrected. "And you are Domenic Trentworth, correct?"

The man's face firmed. "You'll address me as Mr. Trentworth." He puffed his chest. "My place. My rules. Ten bucks an hour. Don't like it, move on and don't waste my time."

Chuck nodded. "Where do you want me to start?"

Domenic walked away, one hand pointed to a closet door. "Broom's in there. Make yourself useful."

Within the hour, Chuck had swept every inch of the building, learning the layout as he moved from one section to the next. He'd found some glass cleaner and towels right when Brandi wandered in.

"Hey, Chuck. How's it going?" She removed her helmet and shook her head to loosen the cropped red curls.

"Good morning." His eyes automatically traveled to the clock on the wall.

The reflective action didn't slip past Brandi. "Yeah, I overslept. Where's Domenic?"

Mr. Trentworth, Chuck reminded himself. "He went through the double doors over there." He wasn't sure what was beyond the doors, but he imagined it was an office.

Brandi tossed her helmet to Chuck. He caught it before it crashed into the display case. "Good catch, Bud." She laughed, ignoring the bold *Private* sign, and disappeared from sight, just like Domenic had done more than an hour before.

By ten o'clock, all the glass cabinets and cases were dust free. One by one, other employees had arrived and introduced themselves. They wore identical shirts with the Consolidated Gold Mine logo displayed over a pocket, and khaki-colored pants.

A tall, slender gentleman, appearing to be about Chuck's age, approached him.

"The name's Bernie." He stuck out a calloused hand and gripped Chuck's. "New hire?"

"Yes. Chuck Hansen. Nice to meet you."

"You do all this cleaning?"

"Had to do something. Not sure what I'll be doing the rest of the day." Chuck pulled a worn handkerchief from his pocket and wiped his brow. "Mr. Trentworth's a man of few words."

Bernie shook his head and muttered something inaudible. "You'll be working with me showing all the city folks how to pan for gold. First three days for training, then you're pretty much on your own. I expect you to be prompt and treat folks with respect." He motioned for Chuck to follow him to a cabinet where he took out a crisp blue shirt and handed it to Chuck.

"You can put this on right over yours. Should fit you, it's the same size I wear."

"Thanks." Chuck unbuttoned the shirt and slipped it on over his pocket T-shirt. "Panning for gold, huh? I've been looking forward to seeing how it's done."

"Yep. Been at it since I was old enough to walk."

"That's a long time. Ever found anything worth keeping?" The child inside Chuck couldn't help but think it was possible.

"That's how this place started. My granddaddy found one of the biggest pieces of pure gold in this state."

Chuck's eyes widened. "I'm confused. Is this your business? I thought Domenic—Mr. Trentworth—owned this place?"

Bernie pressed his shoulders back and raised his chin. "Mr. Bernard Trentworth III at your service."

"Then who is this Domenic fellow?"

Bernie's posture faltered. "My nephew. Another story for another time." He motioned for Chuck to follow. "We've got to get you ready for those customers gathering outside. They're wanting a shot at finding a fortune, too."

Chapter Sixteen

Marge checked her email every day, anticipating the ancestry results from the DNA sample she'd submitted. The extra expense to have the process expedited seemed worth it, yet her patience waned as another day passed without word.

Keeping the rumor from the strange phone call from her sisters created more anxiety than she'd anticipated. Mutzi questioned her nearly every day, wanting to know more about the real reason for the testing. Rose Ellen, scheduled to arrive in town today, would be worse than Mutzi when she realized Marge had withheld something. And she would find out. If Marge didn't accidently let it slip, Mutzi would be sure to tell her sister there was something else going on. She needed answers soon, although she wasn't sure what she'd do with the information once she had it.

"George, did I do the right thing?" As her anxiety grew, so did her doubt. "Honey, is that what this is? An old tale someone once heard and now it's resurfaced?" Marge stared at his picture waiting for an answer. He maintained the same smile, without any hint of responding.

The mysterious phone call had revealed fragmented bits of information, pieces of memories someone shared on her deathbed. It was all Marge had, yet it compelled her to dig further. She needed to validate or refute the story she'd been told. Still, she worried how it would affect their family. *Trust your heart.* A quiet whisper—the reassuring intuition she relied upon when George didn't provide it—had kept her poised, but as time dragged on, it faded.

The grandfather clock in the hall chimed twelve times. Marge turned off the computer and headed to the kitchen. Ashley's class ended soon, her last final of the semester, and together, they were going to spatchcock their first chicken. They'd laughed so hard when they heard the term on a televised cooking show, she'd almost wet her pants. Ashley challenged Marge to try it. The girl's unbounded spirit made everything seem possible. She decided to surprise her protégé while proving to herself it's never too late to learn new things.

Mentally reviewing the time it would take for Ashley to arrive, she watched the clock and pulled the poultry from the fridge just as she heard the front door open.

"School's out," Ashley announced. "Yippee!"

The joyful voice was accompanied by the thud of books landing on the hall table, a sound Marge had grown fond of hearing.

"Congratulations. First year of college is behind you."

The vibrant young woman grabbed an apron from the hook. "What are we fixing for dinner? I know you've come up with something special to celebrate Rose Ellen's homecoming."

Marge grinned and watched Ashley's face light up when she saw two chickens on cutting boards waiting to be dissected.

Ashley squealed. "You are getting bolder every day! Good for you." She headed to the sink to wash up. "So where do we start?"

Marge picked up kitchen shears and nodded to Ashley to do the same. "Breast side down and start with the thigh end."

Once their victims were positioned the same and they'd made the first cut, Marge turned her piece around. "Now do the other side the same way and then remove the backbone."

"I bet you're going to make stock out of it, right?"

"Absolutely."

Ashley watched as Marge worked one hand alongside the cut breast and pulled at the bone with her other hand, easily freeing it. When she finished,

Ashley gave it a try. She fumbled with the slippery hunk and when she tried to pull out the bone, the whole thing flew across the island. Marge caught it before it hit the floor and they both burst into laughter.

"Nice catch." Ashley wiped her hands on a towel and retrieved her wayward chicken. "Let me try that again with dry hands." She managed to remove the bone on the second attempt.

"That's the worst part." Marge chuckled again. "I think these chickens have had their last flight, for sure." She flipped the fleshy meat over and flattened it, pressing on the area where the breastbone had been. Ashley followed her lead. "That's it. We've successfully spatchcocked our chicken. Oh goodness, that sounds so silly."

"It does, but they said it reduces the roasting time and makes the skin crispier."

"That's what they say. We shall see."

Ashley picked up the garlic cloves and held them up. "I love smashing these little things." She laid her cleaver flat against one and smacked it with the palm of her hand.

"They are kind of fun." Marge prepped hers. Under the skin, they added salt, pepper, butter, thyme, and lemon juice before placing the poultry into the oven.

"How are your plans coming for Rose Ellen's birthday party on Sunday? Did you decide where to have it?"

Marge released an exaggerated sigh. "Finally. We're going to have it at Mutzi's house, in the side yard. There's plenty of room and lots of shade trees."

"Wow. That's great. I love their place. It's like being in a park. Bet the flowers are all blooming."

"It is quite lovely." Marge washed her hands and began prepping the vegetables for dinner. "I gave Mutzi control over the decorating, encouraging her to keep in mind it's Rose Ellen's day. It's the first time I'm not in charge of a gathering. I hope everything goes smoothly."

"I bet it will be great. By the way, did you get the results from your DNA test?"

The intuitive young woman had read Marge like a book. "Not yet. The longer I wait, the more confused I get. I'd hoped to have this resolved before Rose Ellen returned."

"Everything happens for a reason, Miss Marge. It's all part of a bigger picture we don't get to see until it unfolds." Ashley wrapped her arms around Marge's waist and hugged her. "It's all going to work out as it should. Don't worry."

Marge couldn't ignore the nagging concern it wouldn't.

Chapter
Seventeen

After their ride on the Vespa, Brandi called Sam's house to talk with Chuck three times. He'd been surprised to hear from her. As their conversations deepened with each call, he detected a softer, less confident side of the young woman who needed reassurance. Perhaps she saw Chuck as someone with whom she could confide.

The confident, almost daring persona Brandi sported masked a still-unsure teenager. The attention of a wealthy young man made her feel special, and she enjoyed the tease, yet she didn't seem ready for more. She liked to dance around the fire ring, but she told Chuck she'd never stepped into the circle.

The weather forecast Sunday night called for heavy rains on Monday. Chuck called the Vespa rider to offer her a drier mode of transportation, which she eagerly accepted.

Sure enough, the heavy downpour started before dawn. Chuck found his way to Marge's house without any trouble. Brandi hurried out the door and down the steps, holding a plastic bag over her head.

"Good morning."

"Hey. Thanks for giving me a lift. Wouldn't have been too fun on my scooter this morning."

"No problem. If it wasn't for you, I wouldn't have a job."

Brandi tugged on the seat belt, adjusting it. "I'm glad I don't have to fight with these things every day. Had the same problem in Nic's car."

The comment surprised Chuck and he turned to Brandi, unsure what to say. "Domenic? You went out with him?"

She turned her face away and peered out the window. "He called a couple times, wanting to see me. I figured, how many times will I have the chance to ride in a Maserati?"

Chuck gripped the steering wheel, trying to focus on the wet road, his mind reeling from the unsettling images he conjured in his mind.

As if she sensed his disappointment she added, "We didn't do anything. He drove me around some backroads to show me how fast it goes and how it hugs the curves."

"Please be careful. The guy's a lot older than you and may not have the same intentions."

Brandi rolled her eyes. "I think I can handle him. Besides, he's my boss. He wouldn't do anything stupid."

The possibilities of things the man could do made Chuck's head spin. "Take it slow, Brandi. Boss or no boss, my gut says this guy doesn't have your best interests at heart."

Chuck pulled the car close to the front door of the building to allow Brandi to get out.

She unhooked her seatbelt and smirked. "I think you're jealous."

Chuck shook his head. "Too old to be jealous. Worried you're getting into a bad situation."

She jumped out and slammed the door. Chuck drove to the closest empty spot and shut off the engine. Unable to avoid the downpour, he sprinted across the parking lot and hurried inside.

Shaking off as much rain as he could, Chuck made way to his assigned duty station to turn on the water taps. Bernie had shown him how to do it during his training. He'd be in charge of demonstrating how to pan for gold. Sounded like more fun than work to him.

As Brandi walked toward the gift shop, she called out, "See you at lunch, Chuck." No more had the words left her mouth, Domenic appeared by her side and grabbed her by the arm.

"No way." He shot a defiant glare in Chuck's direction, then grinned at Brandi. "You're having lunch with me...and breakfast, too." He pulled Brandi close and tried to kiss her neck.

"Stop it. I told you I'm not that kind of girl." Brandi pulled away and pointed to a display case. "I want to check out the gem stones before the place opens."

Domenic grabbed her hand and raised one brow. "I've got something much better to check out."

Brandi shook her head, but didn't pull away. "You're such a bad boy." She giggled as he urged her to follow him.

The sexual tension between the two made Chuck cringe. He looked away, but listened.

"Where are we going?"

"You'll see. I'd rather show than tell."

The urge to take the man outside and bust his chops grew strong. Chuck looked up and made eye contact with Brandi as they passed, mouthing a fatherly warning. *Be careful.* She nodded and gave him a thumbs up. The two disappear through the door leading to the underground mines.

A half hour later, minutes before the place was due to open, the two emerged from behind the closed door. Domenic went to the front and unlocked the door. A blush-faced Brandi followed him, stopping at the counter and smoothing her tangled hair.

A handful of visitors entered and dispersed throughout the building. Chuck donned a heavy, waterproof apron and prepared to start his first demonstration.

A carrot-top youngster with freckles splashed across the bridge of his upturned nose charged toward him, bumping a mature woman waiting in line.

"Me. Me. I want to pan for gold."

Startled at the sudden commotion, the lady clutched her handbag tight to her generous waist and wobbled on three-inch pumps, trying to regain her balance.

Chuck steadied the woman with one hand and lifted the other to slow the lad. "Whoa there, young man. You'll need to wait your turn."

He released his hold on the woman's arm. "Are you okay, ma'am?"

The boy screeched, his high-pitched voice booming as it bounced off the elevated rock ceilings. Another elderly woman tugging at an embroidered shawl slipping off her shoulder hurried toward them and took the boy's hand. "Dennis. I told you to wait for me."

"Tell him, Grandma. Tell him I want to pan for gold...now!"

"Dennis, behave. You'll get your turn." The woman's cheeks flushed bright pink. "He's a very excited little boy."

The first woman eased her death grip on her purse and nodded. "Probably too much sugar in his cereal this morning. I've got grandchildren, too."

Chuck squatted in front of the overzealous child. "Dennis." He waited for eye contact before continuing. "If you listen to me and watch what I show this lady, then when it's your turn, you won't have to wait, you'll know what to do. Deal?"

A forceful head nod confirmed an agreement. Chuck handed a pan to the first woman and led her to the troughs of water. "Dip the pan deep into the water and fill it with some sand." He demonstrated, lifting up a mixture of grit and murky liquid.

The woman glanced around appearing to decide where to set her purse. Apparently unable to find any other acceptable place, she rested it on her feet. After using a bobby pin to control a strand of curly gray hair, she took the pan, holding it with both hands, and let it slip into the large basin. The instant her hands touched the chilly water she retracted them, dropping the pan to the bottom. "Ooh. That's cold." Sprinkles of water landed on the forehead of the boy who stood close enough to be attached to her leg.

Chuck anticipated another outburst. Instead, the child giggled and reached into the basin wetting his own hand and turning to flick some on his grand-mother.

The portly woman smiled and brushed her hand through the boy's thick curly hair. "How about you move back just a little?"

He took one step back, still giggling and pointing to the wet dots on her dress. "You've got polka dots."

Chuck reached into the trough and retrieved the pan for the woman bringing with it the proper amount of mixture. "Now swirl it gently, then pour off some of the sediment and do it again." He handed it back to her.

The lad stretched his neck to watch. "Why? Why do you swirl it?"

"Because gold is heavier than the sand and it sinks to the bottom."

The woman stopped swishing and looked up at Chuck. "I don't see anything."

"Pour off the stuff that floats to the top. Then get a little more water, swirl it some more, and repeat it until I tell you."

She followed his instructions, then paused again. "This takes a long time. Why not empty the pan and dig some more until you find some gold?"

Chuck shook his head. Instant gratification. A mark of today's thinking, even with older folks. "It is a slow process. It takes about fifteen minutes to expose the flakes. You won't ever get to the gold if you keep refilling the pan."

The young boy spoke up. "What if there isn't any when you get to the bottom?"

Chuck winked at him. "I promise. You'll leave here with some." The small sniffer bottle each person received at the end always contained at least a fleck or two of gold.

Once the first woman finished and dried her hands, Chuck reached across the trough and offered a pan to the young boy.

The grandmother squinted her eyes, studying Chuck's face. "You look familiar. Do I know you?"

Chuck's stomach tightened. "Don't believe we've met." He directed his attention to the eager kid whose arms were too short to reach the bottom of the trough. "Let me help you."

"I can do it myself."

Chuck held up both hands. "Okay, tough guy. Show me what you've got," he teased.

The boy stretched on tippy toes and managed to get enough sand in his pan. "See. I can do it."

"You sure can. Maybe you'll be taking my job someday."

The woman tipped her head to the side. "What's your name? Haven't seen you around Dahlonega."

"Chuck Hansen. New to this part of Georgia."

"There's something about your face."

Chuck shook his head. "Been here less than two weeks, ma'am."

The woman persisted. "Is Chuck short for Charles?"

Frustrated with her insistence, but sensing it was useless to avoid her interrogation, he answered. "Middle name's Charles. Given name is Milford."

"Nope. Don't recognize the name. But you look like somebody." The woman tapped a finger on her temple. "I'll ponder it a while. It'll come to me. Thelma Martin never forgets a face."

Just what Chuck needed. Someone too interested in his past.

Chapter Eighteen

The last of the visitors left a few minutes before closing time. Chuck walked to the front of the building and waited for Brandi as she locked a display case and counted the cash in her drawer. He'd been so busy they hadn't had a chance to talk all day.

He took out a handkerchief and wiped his brow. Despite the air conditioned building, he'd worked up a sweat cleaning the panning area. Brandi looked up and noticed him waiting.

"Be there in a minute."

"Thought the heavy rain would keep people away. Sure was wrong."

"Most of them are on vacation. They have to make every day count. Besides, it's dry inside." She zipped the money bag and looked around as if trying to find someone. Her mouth twisted to a frown when her eyes settled on Domenic's office door. She drew in a deep breath. "I need to turn this in."

Chuck sensed the unspoken hesitation. "Want me to come with you?"

"Sure. Whatever floats your boat." Her flippant response was nullified by a renewed glow to her ruddy cheeks.

Brandi walked to the door and pulled on the handle, but it didn't budge. She rapped hard and called out, "Hey. Open the door, unless you want me to keep your money."

The door flung open and the man's eyes skimmed past Brandi straight to Chuck who stood a couple feet behind. An oversized computer screen on the massive mahogany desk revealed he'd been playing a poker game. *Explains the locked door.*

Domenic stepped toward Brandi and closed the door behind him. He glared at Chuck. "What's he still doing here? I told you I'd give you a ride home."

Chuck didn't wait for Brandi to respond. "She booked a round trip ticket with me. I'm taking her home."

The look on Brandi's face was a mixture of relief and angst. "Sorry, Domenic. I'll ride with Chuck tonight."

The response seemed to irritate the man. "Whatever." He grabbed the money bag and walked toward the entrance without a word.

The moment Chuck and Brandi walked out, the door slammed shut behind them and Chuck heard the bolt click. Brandi hurried across the lot and jumped in the car. The palpable tension continued as she buckled her seat belt.

"Long first day," Chuck said.

When she didn't respond, he tried again. "How about we celebrate our first full day on the job with some pizza? I heard Gustavo's is pretty good."

Brandi tested him. "I could use a cold beer."

Chuck grinned. "Sure," he said, playing along. "An icy root beer sounds good."

She rolled her eyes. "You're no fun."

Chuck found a parking place in the town square and they ventured into the pizzeria. He asked for a corner booth and they were seated. The waitress took their order for two salads, a hand-tossed meat lovers fourteen inch, and two drinks.

As they waited for their meals, Brandi stared out the window, seemingly deep in thought.

"Want to talk about whatever's bugging you?"

She continued to look away but spoke, her voice a near whisper. "Why do men have to be such jerks?"

The question made him smile as he thought about his response for a moment. "Not all of them are, but there's enough that it ruins it for the rest of us."

He paused, then decided to add some advice. "Don't take this wrong, but you have to be careful with the messages you send."

"What are you saying?" Her voice escalated, drawing the attention of a couple at a nearby table. "It's *my* fault that my boss wants to grope me?"

The waitress delivered their sodas and hurried away.

Chuck rubbed his forehead. "Look. All men should respect women. Bottom line. But the reality is, not all guys do. Some take advantage of them. A man worth your time will see you as a partner, value you for your intelligence, and appreciate your strengths. It shouldn't be a power struggle."

Brandi released a deep sigh and played with her straw. "When my parents are around, I watch them. Dad's the boss. Always. He's not mean to my mother, but she does everything he wants. Sometimes, I want to scream at her to make a decision, to do something that pleases her, not him."

She put her elbow on the table and leaned on the palm of her hand. "I don't want to be like that, but isn't that what guys expect?"

Chuck set his drink down. "Sometimes parents teach their kids things without even realizing they're doing it. Take your Mom. She probably learned it from her mother. There's nothing wrong with doing things to please a partner, but it shouldn't diminish the relationship or the individual. It's really all about respect. We teach people how to treat us."

Brandi closed her eyes. "So, I should expect Domenic to respect me."

"Absolutely. If he doesn't, send him on his way. You deserve better."

Brandi quieted, as if in deep contemplation.

The delicious aroma of oregano and baked cheese filled the air as the waitress returned with their food. They both stuffed their faces in silence, famished from working all day.

When Brandi finished the last slice, she wiped her face with her napkin. "So how should I handle the jerk?"

Her frankness made Chuck laugh. "Be firm with what you want. If you don't like him pawing at you, tell him so, and stand your ground. There are other jobs with bosses who know how to treat their employees."

"I guess."

"You control most everything else you do. Don't let this guy or any other take your power. Trust me, there are plenty of them out there who would cherish a strong, beautiful woman like you."

She blushed. "You think I'm pretty?"

This time Chuck rolled his eyes. "You have beauty, brains, and a big heart. Believe in yourself and never—never allow someone to kill your spirit."

He stood and took out his wallet, grateful Sam gave him a little extra cash to help out until his first paycheck arrived. "I've assigned you homework for the summer semester. Decide who you want to be and don't settle for anything less."

"Ha. I'm going to ace it. You watch and see."

"I bet you will."

Chapter Nineteen

One last phone call finalized the preparations for Rose Ellen's seventieth birthday party. Marge rechecked her list once again and then tucked it in her apron pocket. "All set for Sunday, George." She stood near the desk and blew a kiss toward his picture.

"And we're all ready for tonight's dinner, Mr. George." Ashley giggled as she yawned and stretched her arms. She winked at Marge and headed to the kitchen where she grabbed her apron.

"You must think I'm a little crazy talking to him."

"Nope. Not at all. Whatever brings you comfort and peace, you should do it." She stood at the sink, washing her hands. "Like me taking an afternoon nap. Now that was peaceful. I haven't done that since I started college."

Marge moved into the dining room and began setting the table for six. "We've got about an hour before Mutzi and Sam arrive." She opened a linen drawer and took out a white tablecloth. "Rose Ellen and Roberto's plane landed a little while ago, so they should be here soon."

Ashley joined Marge in the dining room and opened the velvet covered silverware box sitting on the side table. She stroked the soft burgundy material and sighed. "My grandmother had one of these, too. We only got it out when there was special company."

Marge paused and tilted her head. "I used to do that, wait to use it on specific occasions. Then I decided, my sisters and I are special too."

She wasn't sure when that revelation had come to her, perhaps after George passed. So many things were left unsaid, she didn't want to feel the guilt again. Perhaps it explained why she talked to his picture every day.

When Marge finished setting the plates and glassware on the table, she turned to Ashley. "I really appreciate you taking over the kitchen duties tonight. It's nice to have someone who shares my interests and likes to entertain."

"You've taught me so many things. I'm happy to do it. Besides, you deserve a night off catching up with your sisters." She looked at the table and counted on her fingers. "You said Chuck wasn't coming, so the sixth chair is for George, right?"

Normally the extra chair would be for George, but tonight Marge had decided to break tradition. "It's for a special guest." She waited for Ashley's response.

"Ooh. Who else is coming?"

Marge admired the young woman more every day. *So unassuming.* "They are already here." She paused and smiled. "It's for you, if you'd like to join us, of course"

Her eyes widened and shined with moisture. "I—I would love to." Her voice cracked as if she were going to cry. "I never..."

The unexpected emotions surprised Marge. "You never what?"

Ashley blinked, trying to keep tears at bay. "Our parents hosted many dinner parties for their sophisticated clients, but never for our family. I—I've never eaten in our formal dining room."

Marge tried to imagine having any room that was off limits to family or friends. It made her appreciate the way she was raised. "Oh, honey, I'm sure your parents meant well. They probably thought you'd be bored with business discussions and adult conversations."

"I guess." The sparkle faded from Ashley's eyes. "My sisters and I were expected to stay in our rooms, out of sight, and not make a sound." She wiped a tear that trickled down her cheek. "I always wondered if they really meant to have children. We seemed such a bother to them."

Marge moved closer and wrapped an arm around her shoulder. "Sometimes we misunderstand our parents. They do the best they can with what they know. I'm sure they love all of you."

She took hold of Ashley's shoulders and smiled. "Tonight, you eat with the adults."

"After I serve the food." The glow returned to her precious face. She pressed her shoulders back and smiled. "I'm excited. My first dinner party. I better check on the food."

She pivoted and hurried to the kitchen. Marge followed close behind. Ashley turned around and put a hand up. "Nope, you're off duty. I'm taking it solo from here."

The words made Marge chuckle. "I like your self-confidence. I think you've got this." The doorbell rang as she removed her apron and hung it up. She walked to the foyer, and opened the door for Mutzi and Sam to come in. "I can't believe you didn't let yourselves in."

"Didn't seem like the right thing to do. Besides, you better knock if you come to our place. Never know what we might be doing." Mutzi wiggled her brows and glanced at Sam.

Marge shook her head and laughed. "You're looking great." The bright yellow-checkered smock and purple paisley pants mimicked the joy in Mutzi's face. "Married life agrees with you."

"Most of the time."

Sam smiled as he handed Marge a bottle of wine. "Thank you for having us."

"Wouldn't be a home-coming if family wasn't here."

"Something smells good. What's cooking?" Mutzi drew a deep breath through her nose and hurried toward the kitchen.

Before Marge could answer, Mutzi walked right into Ashley.

"Hi, Miss Mutzi." She held a wooden spoon in midair.

Mutzi took a step back and studied the girl, her eyes settling on what used to be Mutzi's apron. "Don't tell me Marge let you near her stove."

"Not only did I give her full access to the kitchen, she prepared our entire meal for this evening," Marge said coming up behind Mutzi.

Ashley beamed. "Of course, Miss Marge supervised."

Mutzi scrunched her mouth and poked her sister's arm. "You wouldn't let me cook when I lived here."

Marge shook her head. "Once was enough. Besides, I'm pretty sure you liked it that way."

Mutzi rolled her eyes and a smirk inched across her face. "Just because I almost burned the place down—one time." She started to lift a lid on a pot and Ashley stopped her.

"No peeking, please."

The directive surprised Mutzi. She turned to Marge with raised brows. "She's kinda bossy. Did you teach her that, too?"

Before Marge could respond, Ashley spoke up, "No, I'm managing the kitchen. There's a difference. Chefs manage. Tyrants boss."

"She's got spunk. Good for her." Mutzi moved out of the kitchen and started to head toward the study. "When are you going to tell me why you really sent for the DNA test?"

The question made Marge cringe. She'd hoped to avoid the discussion tonight. Ignoring the interrogation, she nodded to Ashley suggesting, "I think it's time to open a bottle—"

"Ciao sono qui" A familiar voice called out in Italian from the foyer.

With all the commotion in the kitchen, Marge didn't hear her other sister come in. She turned toward the foyer calling for Mutzi to follow her.

"Rose Ellen, Roberto! We're so happy you're back in town." Marge wrapped her arms around her sister and squeezed, then stepped back. "You are stunning."

She stood back and admired the ankle length cornflower blue skirt and white linen blouse. "You look fantastic."

"Don't I?" Rose Ellen twisted at the waist making the skirt swirl. "Do you like my new look? I think it makes me look younger."

"It's lovely." Marge glanced at Mutzi to see her reaction. Her twin rolled her eyes and smiled.

"Wait until you see all the new clothes I bought. I'm modaiolo." Rose Ellen turned to Roberto. "That means fashionable, right honey?"

Roberto grinned. "Yes. You are modaiolo, my belissima signora."

Rose Ellen fanned herself and closed her eyes for a moment. "He stills makes my heart flutter."

The strong attraction between the two of them still amused Marge. It had been so many years since Rose Ellen dated, much less shown interest in a man.

Barely taking a breath, Rose Ellen continued, "And guess what. I bought all of us the most luxurious leather jackets and stylish jeans. They are exquisite. I want a picture of all three of us wearing them together."

Leather jackets and jeans? The image tickled Marge. While she enjoyed wearing trendy new clothes, getting Mutzi to relinquish her quirky, colorful style for even one day might take some strong encouraging. But Marge had seen many changes in her twin during the past year. Come to think of it, she was wearing jeans the day she rode Brandi's Vespa.

From the corner of her eye, Marge noticed Ashley signaling to her. She picked up on the gesture. "Perhaps we should move to the dining room and let our chef finish her preparations."

"You've hired a chef to welcome me home?"

"It's Ashley. I told you about her. She's become quite the culinary apprentice."

Ashley set the spoon down and wiped her hands on her apron. "Nice to finally meet you, Ms. Rose Ellen." She extended her hand.

When Rose Ellen didn't immediately accept the offer, Roberto stepped forward and lifted her hand, kissing it lightly. "It's a pleasure to meet you, Ashley."

Not to be overlooked, Rose Ellen placed her hand on top of the two. "Yes. I remember Marge told me you liked to cook."

Ashley withdrew her hand. "I hope to be as good as she is someday." She stepped back and cleared her throat. "If you'll have a seat, we'll get started. Tonight's menu is spatchcock chicken, garlicky Parmesan sweet potatoes, green bean almondine, and glazed carrots."

Marge grinned, proud of the young woman for taking charge. She led the way to the dining room making sure the others followed.

Once they were seated, Ashley presented a bottle of wine. "Tonight I selected a Gérard Bertrand Côte des Roses 2018, a light, fruity, rosé."

Rose Ellen turned her head toward Marge. "I'm impressed."

Marge watched as Ashley poured the strawberry-colored liquid into each glass. "She's going to make a remarkable chef, I can see it already."

"Would have thought she'd be majoring in history since she likes to dig up bones." Mutzi scrunched her face, narrowing her eyes as she turned to Rose Ellen. "Did you know Ashley's helping our sister research our ancestry?"

Rose Ellen clasped her hands together. "Yes, and I'm very excited about it. Did you get the results yet?"

Marge closed her eyes and released a sigh. "Not yet, but I will let both of you know when I hear something." She shot a glare at Mutzi hoping to encourage her to drop the subject, then turned back to Rose Ellen.

"Tell us about your trip. I'm anxious to hear about all the places the two of you visited."

More than willing to oblige, Rose Ellen provided a nearly daily itinerary of their visit to France and Italy.

The frown Mutzi directed toward Marge revealed frustration, but at least for now, the pressure to talk about the unresolved issue had eased.

Chapter Twenty

Mutzi kept Sam and Chuck busy all week with the preparations for Rose Ellen's party. Marge had entrusted her with hosting the event, surprising and pleasing her. She wanted the opportunity to show her sisters a side of her they hadn't seen.

Even though the gathering would be held outside under large shade trees, Mutzi scrubbed and cleaned every surface of their ranch home, as if getting ready for an inspection.

Chuck was assigned the task of painting the dog house and making sure all the "land mines" were cleaned up before guests arrived.

If the weather had cooperated, the tables and chairs would already be in place. The rain storm during the night put a small, but manageable, kink in Mutzi's schedule. Fortunately, Mutzi never trusted the forecasters. They'd predicted sunny skies all weekend, but she noticed there was no dew on the grass Saturday morning, a sure sign of rain by night-fall. The rooster's crow late in the evening confirmed her intuition. She'd made the right decision not to set up until Sunday morning.

Mutzi handed Sam a colored laminated printout of the area where the party would take place. "Here's what it's going to look like."

His eyes grew wide. "Holy cow. You did this? It's amazing."

The photo showed every intricate detail of her plan. Four round tables and two long oblongs in the center would be decorated with white linens. Silver serving dishes were to be used for the catered food. At each of the other four tables were six chairs, fitted with silver and cream colored slipcovers. A large bow draped down the back of every chair.

Mutzi had found similar covers online and offered to buy them, but Marge, her talented seamstress twin, insisted on making them instead. Marge's efforts did not disappoint. They'd add a touch of sophistication to the celebration Rose Ellen would appreciate.

The elegant floral centerpieces she planned to grace the middle of the tables were Mutzi's creation. Sam had driven her to Allyson's Flower Shop on Saturday to pick up dozens of white roses and yellow calla lilies.

When he saw the flowers, his eyes lit up. "Rose Ellen is going to be blown away. She'll love your color choices."

Mutzi wrinkled her nose. "Took everything I had to keep from throwing some lime green and hot pink in there somewhere. Too bland for my taste."

Sam passed the picture to Chuck and gave Mutzi a peck on her cheek. "I can't believe the transformation. Our humble yard is going to look like it belongs in a designer magazine."

Chuck nodded. "He's right." His brows drew tight with a serious thought. "Maybe you should start your own business. You could call it Mutzi's Magical Memories."

Her face flushed. The kind words pleased her, but compliments always caused her discomfort. Unsure what to say, she tapped her watch and started fussing. "It's only a piece of paper until you two get busy setting up those tables."

Sam chuckled and then, as if planned, both men saluted her. "Yes, ma'am. We're on it."

Mutzi hurried inside to finish arranging the last centerpiece. She found herself humming to a radio tune and thinking about Chuck's suggestion. *Why couldn't I do this for others? Lots of creative ideas on the computer. Plenty of free time on my hands.*

The first stumbling block came to mind. Transportation. She still hadn't learned to drive. It meant depending on Sam to take her everywhere.

"Dang it. I need to take care of that." Perhaps Chuck would let her practice in his jalopy.

The rumble of an engine outside interrupted her thoughts. She peered out the window and read the name on a van parked in their driveway. Wolf Mountain Vineyard Catering. Securing the last rose into the base of her arrangement, she hurried to clean off the counter top, brushing a couple errant leaves into the wastebasket. When she opened the door, the succulent scent of smoked brisket filled the room, making her stomach growl.

The woman carrying the large metal container laughed. "Exactly the reaction we hope people have when we deliver."

"You can bet the birthday girl won't be the first one to sample it." Mutzi wanted to lift the lid right then and take a bite. "I'll help you bring in the rest."

"Thanks, but I've got it. I'll put it on the cart and wheel it in. I just didn't want to take a chance with the beef."

"I'll get the door."

Within fifteen minutes, all the containers were inside and the woman left. Mutzi checked her watch. "Gotta get those tables and chairs covered." She dashed out the door and hurried to the shady party area. To her surprise, the guys had taken care of everything and were sitting on the bench, drinking a beer, and playing with Shadow.

"Guess I lit a fire under you two." She let a giggle escape as she inspected the tables. With a glance in Sam's direction, she teased, "When you two are done drinking beer, I've got more for you to do." She winked as she turned to go back in the house. "There might be an extra sandwich or two waiting for you in the kitchen."

Both men jumped to their feet, sending the dog scurrying around confused at the sudden motion. He dashed under one of the tables.

"Catch him before he destroys everything." Mutzi entrusted them with getting things under control and hurried back toward the house.

Chuck grabbed the mutt and hurried past Mutzi, grabbing the door handle. He set Shadow down and held open the door for her. "After you, ma'am."

She stepped inside, nearly tripping over Shadow. The dog jumped up on a chair and dove toward the food on the table.

Chuck caught him mid-leap and held him tight. "I'll put him on his leash as soon as I get done eating."

"If he wasn't so darned cute I'd be tossing him out the door."

Sam wandered in and the two men sat down at the table, forks in hand, waiting for Mutzi to serve them.

She took her time, taking a sample for herself and tantalizing the guys as she savored the delectable beef.

"You're torturing us," Sam moaned.

"What's it worth? I've got a lot more to do before the party?"

"Whatever you want. Just feed us."

She set the plates in front of them, having added some potato salad and pickles. They chomped away at the food as if they hadn't eaten in days.

"You guys will do anything for food."

Shadow clung to Chuck's leg, begging for a bite. "Just about anything, ma'am." Chuck ignored the pup's efforts, refusing to share table food with the dog. He looked up to see Mutzi staring at him. "I do have my limits."

Chapter Twenty-One

L adies, are you ready yet? We must be going." Roberto called from outside the bedroom door. Still sitting on the edge of the bed in her unmentionables, Rose Ellen folded her arms and shouted through the closed door. "She won't tell me where we're going. How am I supposed to decide what to wear?"

"Belissima signora, whatever you choose will be perfetto."

Marge glared at her sister. "I'm not going to ruin the surprise." She adjusted the waist line of her animal print puff sleeve wrap and smoothed it over the olive green cropped capris she'd chosen. "You may be turning seventy, but you act like a child at times." Infuriated with her indecision, Marge stormed to the closet and whipped out a floral maxi Bohemian dress. "Wear this. It's light and airy—and chic."

The pout faded from Rose Ellen's face. "It is one of my favorite finds." She stood and held it close to her body as she looked in the mirror, admiring what she saw. "I wore it when we walked across the Pont des Art Bridge in Paris."

"Perfetto." Marge tried to imitate Roberto's strong Italian accent. "I'm leaving in ten minutes, with or without you." She turned and left the room.

In truth, they'd be driving separately, but Rose Ellen didn't need to know that—yet. Roberto had arranged the special transportation so they both could enjoy the day without worrying about having a few drinks. Marge made her way to the foyer where Roberto waited.

With an eye roll and a shake of her head, Marge released a deep breath. "She should be here in a few minutes."

Roberto rubbed his hands together and nodded. "Molto bene. The stretch awaits."

"She's going to be so surprised. I can't wait for the day to unfold."

The handsome Italian took Marge's hand and squeezed it. "It will be a remarkable birthday she won't forget."

"I think it will. If she ever decides to..."

"Well, what do you think?" Rose Ellen posed, one hand on her hip and the other waved in the air.

"Ah, you chose my favorite one. Good choice." Roberto released Marge's hand and strode toward Rose Ellen. "She walks in beauty, like the night."

Marge recognized the words from Tennyson's poem. A hint of envy rose inside as she observed the two. *Yes, today will be perfect.*

A knock at the front door made them all turn. The limousine driver stood with his hat in hand, a slight frown wrinkled his face.

"Tom? What's he doing here?" Rose Ellen hurried toward the door and peered past the man. She squealed like a little girl. "A limo...for me? Oh, this is going to be fun."

"Nothing but the best for you, dear sister." Marge introduced Tom to Roberto. "Sorry to keep you waiting. I need to grab our purses and we'll be ready."

A chilled bottle of Veuve Clicqu champagne provided a convenient distraction as Rose Ellen and Roberto rode to Mutzi's. Focused on the silver-haired fox next to her and her glass of bubbly, she hadn't noticed where they were until they drove over the familiar pristine white bridge. A tinge of disappointment flashed through her mind. Her anticipation of her party being held at a fancy restaurant or party hall dimmed. "What are we doing here?"

"Ah, my dear, part of the surprise." Roberto dropped a gentle kiss on her lips.

The limo stopped alongside the house. Instead of the front door, Roberto took her hand and urged her to follow him to the backyard. "This way."

As they rounded the corner of the house, a unified cheer startled her. "Surprise!" Rose Ellen tried to focus on the faces of her guests huddled in a group to her right, but her eyes darted to the dazzling garden scene spread under the magnificent oaks." Her breath caught as her eyes settled on the stunning table settings and silky silver streamers woven through the trees. "Oh, mercy," she breathed. "How absolutely exquisite."

She turned to her sisters. "You two did this for me?" She folded her hands across her chest. "I'm humbled. I truly am humbled."

Marge and Mutzi moved toward her. Entwined in a group hug, the two said, "Happy seventieth, Sis."

"When did you have time to do this, Marge?"

Marge smiled. "This was all Mutzi. She's quite the designer, don't you think?"

Rose Ellen's eyes widened and her mouth fell open as she tried to find words to express her astonishment. "I...I never knew you were so talented." She gazed at the area again. "Everything is so elegant ...and sophisticated."

Mutzi raised a brow and half-grinned. "What? You didn't think I knew what those words meant?" She gave Rose Ellen's hand a squeeze. "Sam and Chuck helped make it happen. Marge made the chair covers, too. But I did design it with you in mind. Just for the record, I want lots of colors and balloons, maybe even clowns, at my seventieth."

The three laughed. Marge nodded toward all the people still standing to the side. "I think you shouldn't ignore your guests any longer.

Almost giddy with the excitement, Rose Ellen hurried to greet friends she hadn't seen in years, sharing all the details of her trip to Italy and France. As she fluttered from one guest to the next, wrapped in Roberto's comforting arm, she caught sight of her daughter and son-in-law walking toward her.

"Happy Birthday, Mom." April hugged her tight. "You look fabulous."

"You made it just in time for dinner." Rose Ellen turned her cheek for a kiss from Paul, who obliged and shook Roberto's free hand.

"We took the earliest flight out of Miami. Fortunately, the plane landed on time and we didn't check our bags." April closed her eyes and breathed in. "Something smells wonderful."

Rose Ellen paused, and a heavenly smoky scent filled her nose. "It does. And I'm starving." From the corner of her eye, she observed Ashley, Brandi, and

Marge carrying silver platters toward the tables. "Looks like Marge outdid herself on the food."

"Mutzi told me they had it catered."

"Really?" Rose Ellen shook her head. "I can't believe they did all this for me." Rose Ellen looked around and marveled at the effort they'd put into it. "By the way, how was the law convention?"

Before April could respond, Mutzi appeared by her side and grabbed Rose Ellen's arm. "Time to stop talking. Let's eat, Sis."

Rose Ellen snickered. "Always the bossy one." She met Mutzi's eyes. "This is unbelievable, Mutzi. Thank you."

"You're welcome. Now let's eat."

Once everyone was seated for dinner, only one empty chair remained next to her sister. Rose Ellen knew it was Marge's way of always remembering George.

Each place setting held a champagne glass, etched with Rose Ellen's name, the date, and a fancy 70. A decorative calligraphy menu balanced on an easel and identified the caterer, Wolf Mountain Vineyard. Rose Ellen picked it up and read. Smoked beef brisket, Yukon potato wedges with smoked paprika, sautéed squash, salad tossed with house dressing, and warm, crusty bread.

Marge stood and raised her glass in a toast. "To Rose Ellen, my sister, my friend. You inspire me with your courage and youthful adventures. May this be just the beginning of another long journey filled with love, laughter, and many blessings."

Everyone joined in, clinking their glasses and offering a cheer. Rose Ellen turned and lost herself in Roberto's deep blue pools, their lips meeting in a dreamy kiss. She closed her eyes, cherishing the heavenly experience.

"People who have more birthdays live the longest." Mutzi interrupted the intimate moment.

It took a few seconds for her words to filter through. "You are so silly." Rose Ellen rose from her chair. "I'm supposed to start the serving line, right?"

Mutzi laughed and did a curtsy. "Yes, Queen Rose. Lead the way."

Chapter Twenty-Two

Most of the guests had left by sundown. Rose Ellen waved goodbye to Ashley and Brandi as they rode off on the Vespa. Her sisters and daughter had cleared the tables and removed all the decorations. Deciding to treasure a few moments to herself, Rose Ellen walked around to the side of the house hoping to catch a glimpse of the full moon. It was something she'd learned to appreciate thanks to Roberto and their trip abroad. The cool crisp air refreshed her tiring body.

She noticed the man's silhouette as he gazed up toward the starlit sky. Curious to hear his story, she decided to join him. "It's a beautiful night, isn't it?"

"Doesn't get much better than this. Reminds me of a few rare moments in Na—another place."

The man intrigued Rose Ellen. "We really didn't get a chance to meet earlier."

He nodded and ran a hand through his hair. Shadow clung close to his side. "Chuck Hansen, at your service, ma'am." He extended his hand and shook hers. "Quite a special day for you. I appreciate being part of it."

"It was very special. I don't know how it could be any better." She shivered, drawing her shoulders tight.

"How about we move over by the campfire? Sam and I set up some chairs earlier. I think he planned on all of you having a quiet moment together."

The blazing campfire helped warm the chill that settled in Rose Ellen's weary bones. "Come sit by me. I want to talk."

She noticed his face harden a bit as he waited for her to settle into a chair, and then he joined her. Rose Ellen studied the high cheek bones and elongated nose. It struck a familiarity that she couldn't assign. "Tell me about yourself, Chuck."

He cleared his throat and released a sigh. "Not much to tell. Just trying to get by." He stared off into the darkness as she waited for more. "Met Sam when I was living in my car. He offered to let me stay here until I got back on my feet."

"Where's your family?"

He withdrew a small pocket knife and fiddled with the blade, clicking it back and forth. "No family. Just me...and my shadow." He released a slight chuckle.

The sadness in Chuck's eyes tore at her heart. Rose Ellen couldn't imagine not having anyone in your life to lean on. After spending many months away from her sisters, she cherished the joy of returning home and having family to greet her. "Have you always been alone?"

Chuck stared at the fire and drew in a slow, deep breath.

"Rose Ellen, where are you?" Roberto's voice called out.

"By the fire, dear." She looked at Chuck and tried again. "I can tell by the things you aren't saying, you've had some rough times."

Chuck squirmed, slipped the knife back into his pocket and stretched his arms. He bent and picked up Shadow, stroking him gently, as he cleared his throat. "No one really wants to hear about someone else's problems. Besides, this is your birthday. You need to focus on more positive things."

Roberto walked toward the fire ring. Sam followed, pulling a rolling cooler. Soon all the family had gathered and claimed a chair.

Chuck stood and excused himself. "I'll let you folks have quiet time together."

Rose Ellen caught his arm. "Please, stay. When we gather, we're all family."

He hesitated and glanced around at the others who nodded in agreement.

Mutzi pointed to a chair. "You get the prize of sitting next to Queen Rose." Her jovial comment brought a roar of laughter.

"Where's my crown? I thought you'd make me one for my birthday."

Mutzi twisted the top off a bottle of beer and placed the cap on Rose Ellen's head. "There you go. You're crowned." Another round of laughter followed.

Rose Ellen grew quiet for a second. "Best birthday ever. Couldn't have wanted anything more. Thanks to all of you for making it so special."

April stood and cleared her throat. Paul joined her. "It's not quite over yet. We didn't give you our present." She took Paul's hand in hers and pressed it to her belly. "You're going to be a grandmother."

The surprising announcement rippled around the circle like water flowing down a creek bed and settled into Rose Ellen's mind. She jumped to her feet, toppling her chair, and rushed to April's side. "I can't believe it. Are you sure? You've been trying for so long, I never thought it would happen."

"Yes, Mom. I'm sure." April squeezed her mother's hand. "She'll be a December baby. What a great Christmas gift, huh?"

"She?" Rose Ellen drew her brows tight. "You know the gender this soon?"

April shrugged and grinned. "Not officially. But I feel it in my heart. We're going to be blessed with a healthy baby girl."

Paul shook his head and frowned. "I think it's going to be a boy, but what do I know."

When Rose Ellen looked around, she realized everyone was on their feet, waiting to congratulate the happy couple. She looked toward Marge and Mutzi, feeling her heart would burst with joy. "I'm going to be a grandmother. We're having a baby and I'm going to spoil it rotten."

"Such delightful news. I'm so happy for all of you." Marge squeezed Rose Ellen's hand.

Mutzi patted her older sister on the shoulder and chuckled. "Cool. Maybe they'll have triplets. One for each of us to spoil."

The suggestion triggered a gasp from April. "Don't even think such a thing!"

The sound of the laughter seemed to echo through Rose Ellen's head and her body began to sway. She felt Roberto's strong arm guide her back to her chair. Someone handed her a bottle of water. Once settled down, Rose Ellen took a sip and the spell passed. "I guess all the excitement and the warmth of the fire got to me."

She fanned herself and looked around as everyone stood staring at her. "Please, sit. I'm fine. Really."

Once they did as she'd requested, Rose Ellen said, "It's been such an extraordinary birthday. You have truly made me feel like a queen." She shook her head. "It couldn't get any better than this."

With those words, Roberto stood and moved in front of Rose Ellen. "Bel Fiore, you have made *my* life better since the day we met." He reached into his pocket and withdrew something. With one knee on the ground, he reached out and offered a ring. "I hope you will allow me to make today and every day that follows better for both of us. Will you marry me?"

Rose Ellen swayed again, her head spinning as the crackling fire danced behind Roberto. *Was this a dream?* If it was, she never wanted to wake. Still dazed, she slipped the gold miner ring from her left ring finger and passed it to the person standing closest to her. Extending her trembling hand as a tear trickled down her cheeks, she whispered, "Yes."

Chapter Twenty-Three

Dark threatening clouds filled the skies as Chuck pulled into the gold mining parking lot. He hadn't expected to see Brandi's Vespa parked next to the black Maserati, especially since he'd arrived a half-hour before the place opened. He'd planned to speak to Domenic alone.

Chuck entered the unlocked building and looked around, noticing the boss's open office door. "Anybody here?" With no response, he peered inside the room. His pulse quickened as his eyes scanned the turned over chair and scattered papers. As he turned to leave, his eye caught sight of a crystal paperweight in the corner of the room. A red smear on the object drew him closer and he bent to pick it up, noticing a diminutive trace of similar droplets trail out of the room.

Tossing it back to the carpeted floor, he followed the lead until it ended near the entrance to the mine. His stomach roiled as his mind envisioned a fight between Brandi and Domenic. He pressed his hand on the heavy door, then hesitated. *What am I doing?* For a brief moment, he remembered befriending a woman and being forced to make a similar decision years ago, one which ended badly. He turned away.

Bernie's warning never to enter the mine without a flashlight sent him searching for the first one in sight. He grabbed it and rushed back, pushing through into the dark tunnel. Even with the aid of the fading beam, it took a few minutes for his eyes to adjust. Five minutes into his journey, the light flickered.

"Damn it, don't quit on me now." He tapped the object on the palm of his hand, bringing it back to life for a while. *Should I turn back and get another one?* Fearing each minute lost might make a life or death difference, he pressed forward. He decided to save whatever battery was left and turned off the flashlight. The path faded from sight.

Creeping along the damp passageway, his eyes tried to adjust to the blackness with little success. "Brandi. Are you in here?" His voice quivered from the fear rising up from his gut into his throat. A rock tumbled somewhere in front of him and he stopped. Footsteps? The pounding pulse in his temples made it impossible to hear. After waiting another minute, he moved on, deciding he'd imagined it.

With each step further into the unlit cave, he began questioning his decision. Was he overreacting?

Maybe they aren't even in here. Had he checked all the areas in the building before rushing off like a mad man? No. He hadn't. There were plenty of places he hadn't checked.

Still, his gut told him to keep moving.

Inching forward, he splashed through streams of water retracing the route in his mind, trying to remember which way to turn when he reached a fork in the mine. He took a deep breath and released it slowly as he mentally listened to another warning Bernie shared the day he'd taken him on his first tour. "Right is right." Chuck nodded as the conversation replayed.

Caution tape had blocked the other direction and he heard Bernie's word again. "It's too dangerous that way. Darn shame because there's a huge vein of gold up there." He'd shined the light on it some twenty feet above. It was an image a penniless guy couldn't forget.

Already exhausted from the stress of his questionable mission, Chuck stopped, pulled out a handkerchief and wiped sweat from his forehead. Something plunked to the floor of the cave. He strained his eyes to find the missing object, then turned on the flashlight. It flicked its last beam.

The thumping in his head grew stronger again. He'd only been in the mine once. Going back would be difficult. Moving forward without any light would be nearly impossible. Yet, he knew he'd continue. Something told him Brandi needed him to trust his instincts.

He edged forward, bumping his head on a protruding, jagged rock. He paused and regrouped. When he started again, he spread his hands first, above and to the side, feeling his way along the wall, whenever it was close enough to touch. When it wasn't, he had to trust his own inclinations.

As Chuck made a turn, the yellow tape came into view. He squinted, examining it and noticing one piece of the tape draped over the other, leaving enough room for someone to enter. He quickened his step a half beat, still unable to see more than an inch or two in front of himself.

He'd made about ten steps when his foot hit something pliable on the floor. He bent to examine it more closely. "Brandi!" Her lifeless, half-naked body crumpled in a pile, blood oozing from her head.

Chuck ripped off his shirt and knelt, pressing the wadded cloth to the bleed. Her eyes flickered open and then closed again.

"My leg." No more than the words left her mouth, her body went limp.

His eyes adjusted to the darkness and he saw the bone protruding above her knee. He unbuckled his belt intending to use it for a tourniquet. The oversize pants fell around his knees.

Chuck's feet felt the rumbling before the thunderous boom. Loose rock and dirt crashed around them. He covered Brandi with his own body. Her shrill scream was the last thing he heard before the walls came crashing down.

Chapter Twenty-Four

Bernie Trentworth fussed under his breath as he shoved his key into the lock of the door. "First day off in a month and that good for nothing nephew doesn't show." A dozen employees scurried past him to get to their appointed stations before he allowed the waiting customers to enter. He tipped his hat to those who remained. "Thanks for your patience, folks. Come on in and look around while we open up."

After removing his worn baseball cap and turning on some lights, he noticed the door to Domenic's office was open. He walked toward it and glanced in, then pulled the door shut. Bernie knew he'd hear the wrath of his paranoid nephew, whenever he decided to show up, if he learned anyone had entered his space.

"Excuse me." A young couple, perhaps mid-twenties, stood by the counter nearest the front door, the woman waving to get his attention. "How soon will we be able to pan for gold—and take the tour?"

It was then that Bernie remembered seeing Chuck's car and Brandi's scooter parked in the lot, yet the girl was nowhere in sight. "I don't know. Give me a minute." He grumbled again as he walked away. "She's probably off with that fool nephew of mine." Releasing an exaggerated sigh, he shuffled through the rest of the building looking for her. When he went to the pan sifting area, he realized Chuck was also missing. "Dang it. Where are they?"

He strode from one employee to the next. No one had seen them. It didn't make any sense. Tension traveled up his neck and settled into a headache. Not only was his nephew nowhere to be found, two more employees were missing. "How the hell am I supposed to run a business...?" His voice trailed off as he hurried to find a replacement for Chuck. "Zach, stop what you're doing and get the panning area ready. I'll do the pre-walk-through of the mine before starting the tours."

"Yes, sir. I'm on it."

"And tell Tara to cover the front desk."

"Got it, Boss."

Everyone still respected Bernie as the real person in charge. He appreciated it. Hopefully, one day soon the title of the business would return to its rightful owner. For now, he had to put up with the guy who'd bailed him out of financial trouble.

Grabbing a hard hat and two flash lights, he made his way into the mine, sweeping the beams wide, side to side, in search of any fallen rocks in the path. Couldn't risk another lawsuit. Last year, some dumb kid climbed over a railing and broke his arm. Although there were signs warning people, and the guide had repeatedly asked the parents to watch the child, they took him to court. Lawyer fees and court costs drained every penny of his savings.

About a third of the way through the mine, something shiny caught Bernie's attention. He stopped, bent down, and lifted a gold ring from the wet cave floor. He shined a light on it as he examined it closer, recognizing the unique piece. "I'll be damned. How in the heck did that get here?" Tucking it in a pocket, he continued, kicking a few errant rocks to the side.

As he moved closer to the fork in the cave, the amount of debris increased. He turned the second flashlight toward the ceiling beyond the yellow taped off section. "Crap." A large chunk of the wall had collapsed. "Won't be any tours today." Just what he needed, another big expense, besides losing the income from the mine tours. He'd have to get an excavating crew out to check out the stability before resuming any walkthroughs.

A faint hissing noise made him halt. He shined both lights toward the fallen rocks and listened. The familiar sound reminded him of when his father was on a ventilator fighting for his life. "Somebody in here?"

A muffled groan made Bernie's heart sink. "Who's there? Is that you, Chuck?" Again a deeper moan echoed back. The piles of crumbled rock were more than one man—especially an old man—could move by himself. "Hang on. I'm going for help."

The trip out of the mine was the fastest Bernie had ever made it. He rushed into Domenic's office to call for help, startled to see him sitting at his desk, playing on the computer. "Where the hell have you been?"

"None of your business, old man. Get out of my office."

Bernie ignored the command and picked up the phone, dialing 911. He glared at his nephew as he shouted into the phone. "There's been a collapse in the gold mine. We'll need every hand you can send."

Domenic jumped up from his chair. "Are they dead?"

Bernie's face burned with anger. "They? You knew? What the hell's going on?"

"That Chuck fellow and the girl." Domenic paced, rubbing his hands together. "I thought I could trust them alone while I went back to my place for something."

Something poked at Bernie's brain. Something he couldn't identify. There was more to this than his nephew was telling, but he needed to get back to the mine. Every minute counted.

As he turned to leave the office, Bernie commanded his nephew, "Tell the customers they need to leave. Close it down."

Domenic stepped in front of his uncle, hands on his hip as he spat his response. "I'm the boss, remember? I give the orders around here."

"Then act like one. Do your frigging job. You can bitch at me later." Bernie pushed past him. "I don't have time for your ignorance."

Before heading back into the mine, Bernie grabbed a hard hat with a headlamp, some extra batteries, and a shovel. Loaded with the gear, he made his way back to the site where the two were buried, he began moving boulders one by one, taking his time not to cause more injuries. He called out again and again, but no one answered. The absence of the hissing sound he'd heard earlier suggested it might be too late to save the workers.

Trying to ignore the screaming muscles in his own aging body, Bernie labored as he dug through the rubble. Another fifteen minutes passed before emergency help arrived. They insisted Bernie leave and let them do their jobs. With no energy left to resist, he stepped aside and allowed the men to take over. "I think there's two of them in there. Be careful."

Bernie watched from a distance as they worked through the mounds of rock. When the crew reached Chuck and Brandi, the sheriff ushered Bernie out of the mine.

"They're both unconscious, but still alive. You need to leave so we can get them out."

He waited outside the door until they carried the blanket-covered bodies out on stretchers and followed them to the parking lot where two ambulances awaited. Exhausted and sick to his stomach from the whole ordeal, Bernie decided not to get into it with his nephew. Instead, he'd go home, change clothes, and head to the hospital to check on his new recruits.

All the staff left, as Domenic directed them to, and once Brandi and Chuck were taken away, the place emptied. Only a few first responders remained, making notes and asking questions for their reports.

A young policeman walked into Domenic's office and closed the door behind him. "Need to ask you some questions."

"Terrible accident. Not sure I can help. I wasn't here when it happened."

"What do you know about..."—he looked down at his notepad—"Chuck Hansen?"

"Brandi brought the homeless dude in with her and vouched for him, so I hired him." He pulled open a drawer and took out a file folder, resting his hands on it. "Foolish old man had the hots for the girl. Always hanging around her."

"Is that right?" The cop scratched something on his pad. "Might explain..." he didn't finish his thought.

"What? You know something else. You can tell me."

The young officer looked over his shoulder, then leaned in close. "Looked like he was trying to get a little action. They found him nearly naked on top of her."

Domenic's eyes widened. *Could this get any better? Maybe I'll add some fuel to the fire.* Domenic pulled out a single sheet of paper, being sure to leave the second page concealed, and slipped it to the officer. "This might interest you. His real name is Milford. I ran a security check on him. Just got the results yesterday." He waited a few minutes and then pointed to the bottom of the page. "Spent time in prison for a similar attack. I was going to can him today. Can't have a pervert working for me."

As the officer read the paper, his eyes grew wider. "I'll keep this."

"Go ahead. It's served my purpose."

"Thanks. We'll get this guy back where he belongs, if he lives."

"What about the girl? Is she going to make it?"

"Don't think so. Doesn't look good."

Domenic displayed his best poker face. "Sorry to hear that."

Chapter Twenty-Five

The timer on the oven dinged. Marge pulled out the breakfast casserole and placed it on a hot plate in the middle of the kitchen island. With everything else in place, she called out to her guests. "Breakfast is served." When Rose Ellen and Roberto failed to respond, Marge walked down the hall and called out again.

Roberto stepped out of the bedroom. "I apologize for the delay, my dear fiancée seems to have lost her ring."

"Which ring?"

"The one Daddy commissioned for me. The gold miner." Rose Ellen dug through her purse, tossing everything in it onto the bed. "I must have taken it off when Roberto proposed, but I don't remember what I did with it."

Memories of all the strange things that happened with that ring flashed through Marge's mind. Was it really just a year ago when Mutzi confessed to keeping it from her sister? She drove Marge crazy with her superstitious belief that it was cursed. Almost had Marge believing it, too, given all the bizarre coincidences she'd experienced.

As soon as Marge wore the ring, disturbing incidents occurred. She didn't want to encourage the crazy notion, but how could her brand new tire have blown out while driving the women to Gibb's Gardens. It scared her to death and it cost her a small fortune to fix it and the brakes. And it didn't stop there. Her lovely pencil skirt split, the strap broke on her expensive designer purse, and then she twisted an ankle—it was all too much.

It wouldn't bother Marge if she never saw the ring again, but she knew it meant a great deal to Rose Ellen. "I'm sure it will show up." She helped her sister put the items back in her purse. "Let's enjoy our breakfast before it gets cold."

Roberto's eyes lit and he drew in a deep breath. "I smell Italian sausage and baked cheese. It's making my mouth water." He grinned and took Rose Ellen by the hand. "Perhaps the distraction will help you remember."

"Perhaps." Rose Ellen frowned and followed her fiancé as he tugged her toward the door. "Lord knows you love to eat. I don't know how you stay so trim."

Marge followed behind them. Once they were seated, she served the casserole and passed around the bowl of fruit. She watched as each took a bite and closed their eyes.

"Mmm. Just like I remember. It's delicious." Rose Ellen took another bite.

"This is amazing, Marge." Roberto raised his fork in the air. "Perhaps you should open a bed and breakfast."

The suggestion tickled her. She'd considered it some years ago. Cooking brought her so much pleasure when there was someone to share it with. "I'm glad you're enjoying it."

Her mind drifted off as she thought about how empty the house would be if the triplets returned home over the summer. She imagined Rose Ellen and Roberto had plans to travel more now that the party was over. Having an empty house weighed heavy on her heart.

"I've got it!" Rose Ellen dropped her fork and slapped her hands on the quartz island top. "Chuck. I gave the ring to him. He must have kept it." Her face firmed and she drew her brows close. "I need to find him before he hocks it."

"Rose Ellen. What a terrible thing to say." Marge tossed her napkin on the counter. "Just because a man's down on his luck doesn't mean he's a thief."

"Well, what do we really know about him?"

"We know that Sam trusts him enough to invite him to stay in his home."

Rose Ellen rolled her eyes. "Sam's such a nice guy, he'd invite a felon to stay with him."

"I'm sure the man has no intention of stealing your precious ring." The bitter words flew out Marge's mouth. Regret followed them. "I'm sorry. I know how sentimental you are about the ring." She released a sigh. "For me, it stirs so many unpleasant memories, I'd just as soon forget."

The room went silent. Marge watched Rose Ellen's face as her bottom lip pressed forward into a pout. "It *was* terrible when April wrecked her car, and broke off her engagement to Paul." The pout changed to a half smile. "And it was kind of funny when I bumped into the china cabinet and it crashed to the floor. I know you didn't think so."

"No. It wasn't funny. A lot of my dishes broke and it almost landed on top of me."

"But it didn't and you found some matching plates at the antique store. So no real harm was done."

"True." Marge reminded herself to focus on the positive, and search for the silver lining.

The ring took them on a journey that changed their lives and strengthened their sister bond. If it hadn't been for the ring, the three sisters may never have shared their true dreams and deep feelings about each other. Marge looked at her sister and smiled. "On the other hand, if it hadn't been for the ring, you wouldn't have met Roberto."

Rose Ellen reached over and patted Roberto's cheek. "The ring wasn't cursed. It brought me love."

Marge had to agree. The good outweighed the bad. "If Chuck has it, I'm sure he'll get it back to you. He's working right now, but you could call Mutzi. Maybe he gave it to her."

"I'll wait until later. Roberto promised to take me shopping in the square." She hopped off the stool and waited for him to rise. "I want to stop at Magical Threads. Maybe I'll make a quilt for my new grand-baby."

"Ah, yes. Another shopping day." Roberto rolled his eyes. "We are going to have to find you another hobby, my dear."

Rose Ellen nudged him with her shoulder. "You are my new hobby." She leaned in and kissed him.

"I'm so happy for you two getting engaged. And April's news about the baby. What a wonderful sur-prise."

"I can't wait. I've waited so long to have a grandchild. Hope it's a girl."

"Doesn't matter, as long as it's healthy." Marge picked up the empty plates and took them to the sink. She couldn't ignore the nagging thought concerning her. Much like Rose Ellen, April had put her career ahead of marriage and children. The decision came with an increased risks of complications. She whispered a silent prayer.

Chapter Twenty-Six

With a trembling hand, Marge removed the papers from the printer. She'd anticipated a sense of relief when the agonizingly long wait ended. All this time she'd been sure the findings would disprove the implausible story and she'd be able to attribute it to the confused memory of a dying woman.

She stared at the document—not understanding—nor believing the information. *Now what do I do?* Marge shut down the computer, folded the papers in half, and slipped them into her pocket. Wandering from the study to the kitchen and back again, she contemplated her next move. Looking up at George's picture, she waited for inspiration. Once again, he didn't fail her.

She grabbed her purse and walked into the foyer, checking her hair in the mirror before heading to her car.

The half-hour drive to the nursing home in Dawsonville did little to settle Marge's anxiety. It wasn't her habit to show up somewhere unannounced, but the situation called for more answers, and she needed them now. She hoped the bed-ridden, retired nurse felt well enough to talk with her. Hearing the woman's story in person might provide a clearer picture regarding one of the outcomes from the DNA testing, but the other one surprised and puzzled her.

Marge parked the car and went into the lobby of the facility. After signing the visitors' log, the woman at the desk directed her down a long hall to room 1021. Marge removed a tissue from her purse and dabbed at her damp forehead. The door of the woman's room was open. Marge lingered in the hallway and studied the thin frame sitting up in bed, staring out the window. What in the world was she going to ask her? She racked her brain trying to decide what to say as she gathered her courage.

As if sensing someone watched, the white-haired woman turned her head toward the door. "Come in."

Marge drew in a breath and entered. "Thank you."

The frail lady adjusted the colorful patchwork quilt covering her legs. Faded blue eyes sparkled in the sunlight beaming through the window, revealing a weathered, but still beautiful, face.

"I'm sorry to bother you." Marge stood on the far side of the bed. "I'm Margaret Ledbetter.

The woman's cheeks rose with a broad smile. "Ah, yes. I've been expecting you."

"You have?"

"My granddaughter, Geraldine, told me she'd talked with you."

"She did. I've been waiting for—" Marge paused, unsure if the woman would understand the contemporary terminology.

"Ancestry DNA results." She smiled. "I don't blame you. I would have done the same." The woman patted the end of the bed. "Come sit."

Marge moved closer and balanced her bottom on the corner, trying not to disturb the woman. "I'm so confused. I don't understand how this kind of thing could happen." She folded her hands across her purse. "Geraldine says you have information that might explain it. Do you feel up to talking with me?"

She leaned back on her pillow and closed her eyes for a moment. "You almost waited too long. My days are numbered by hours." A coughing spell took the woman's breath and she sat up, struggling to recover.

Alarmed, Marge stood. "Perhaps another day would be better."

"No." She regained her composure and laid her head back again. "I've carried this secret long enough."

Marge waited, unsure whether she should stay or not.

The woman opened her eyes and took a deep breath. "Sit. I must tell you—now." She reached out her hand toward Marge.

Marge held it as the distressing story flowed from the woman's lips like spilled ink on paper. She listened in silence, watching the fine lines around her eyes deepen as she recalled each unconventional detail. She watched the torment of regret release from the woman's face as she explained her reasons for hiding the secret so long. It left no doubt she spoke the truth.

"Thank you for being brave enough to share this with me. A new chapter unfolds for our family. One we'd never know if you hadn't spoken the truth."

A peaceful sigh released the tight wrinkles from the woman's eyes, and her breathing slowed. As Marge stood to leave, the woman smiled. "Thank you for letting me make things right. I'm ready for the Lord now."

Chapter Twenty-Seven

The bell on the Magical Threads door tinkled as Rose Ellen walked into the shop. Roberto had dropped her off on his way to Woody's Barber Shop. "Hello?" She walked down an aisle in search of assistance.

"Be with you in a minute," a voice called out from behind a mound of fabric.

Rose Ellen ran her hand over a bolt of butterfly enhanced cotton material. "Bet Mutzi would love this."

"I'm sure she would, Rose Ellen." Thelma waddled closer, nodding her head.

"You remembered my name?" Rose Ellen raised her left hand and stroked her face, letting her fingers linger at her neck, posing as she hoped the light made her new brilliant diamond flicker.

"I never forget a name nor a face." She lifted a bundle of fabric and refolded it, smoothing out the edges, and tucking it on a shelf next to a similar pattern. "Got a new ring, too. What'd you do with the gold miner one?"

A frown replaced the smile on Rose Ellen's face. "I think the guy staying with Mutzi and Sam has it." She pressed her lips tight, sorry she shared that bit of information to the town gossip lady.

"I'm surprised they'd let a felon stay with them." Thelma glanced up for a second to catch Rose Ellen's reaction and then continued to arrange the bolts of fabric.

Rose Ellen tried to stifle a gasp. "I'm sure you're mistaken. Perhaps you're confusing him with someone else."

Thelma shook her head. "Nope. Same guy. Met him at the gold mine when I took my grandkid there. Looked kinda familiar, so I checked him out. His real name is Milford Charles Hansen. He did time for raping a young girl."

The words sucked the air from Rose Ellen and she reached out to steady herself. Could this guy really be a felon? Was her sister in danger having him under the same roof? Would she ever see her daddy's ring again? Anxious to talk with Mutzi, she turned to leave, then realized she had no transportation until Roberto came back for her.

Thelma smirked like a cat who snagged a canary. "What did you come in for today?"

Rose Ellen thought for a moment and remembered. "A baby quilt. I'm going to be a grand-mother."

The heavy-set woman stopped fussing with the bolts of fabric and turned. "Well, how about that. I thought April was too old, but I guess I was wrong."

This woman knew how to stir the pot, but Rose Ellen decided not to let her steal her thunder. "My sisters threw an absolutely exquisite birthday party for me yesterday. Too bad you weren't there. The catered food was delicious." She didn't know why the two of them poked at each other, but Thelma wasn't going to get the best of her. "April and Paul surprised me with the announcement there, right before Roberto proposed."

Thelma forced a smile and nodded, avoiding any congratulatory praises. "Follow me. I have the perfect baby quilt, good for either sex."

As Thelma busied herself digging out the bolt of material, Rose Ellen continued to share every detail of her party and the proposal.

Thelma listened and nodded as she cut the fabric, then led Rose Ellen to the cash register, grabbing matching thread as they passed the display.

The doorbell tinkled and Roberto walked in as Rose Ellen prepared to pay. He wrapped an arm around her waist and planted a kiss on her cheek.

Roberto blocked the credit card in Rose Ellen's hand as she handed it to Thelma. "I'll take care of it, my dear. Did you get everything you needed?"

Rose Ellen grinned. "Such a gentleman." She turned to Thelma. "This...is my fiancé, Roberto Montelini."

Thelma reached out to shake his hand. When he lifted it to his lips, Rose Ellen saw the woman's knees buckle. The pink flush in her cheeks matched the gingham checkered smock she wore.

Rose Ellen winked. "And he's all mine." She wiggled her ring finger flashing the diamond again.

Thelma poked back again, "Don't forget to tell Mutzi I said hello. Hope you get your other ring back."

The mention of Mutzi killed Rose Ellen's buzz. She whipped out her cell phone and dialed her sister as they walked to the car. After a dozen rings, she hung up. "Well, shoot."

"Is everything all right?"

"Oh, that woman told me the most awful news. She said the man staying with Mutzi is a felon. I wanted to ask Mutzi if she knew, and if she has my ring, but she's not answering her phone."

Roberto waited for Rose Ellen to get in the car. "That's concerning news about Chuck. Do you think it's true?"

"Knowing Thelma, it probably is. She seems to know everyone's business."

"Do you want to drive over there?"

Rose Ellen shook her head. "If she was home, she would have answered. I'll talk to her later."

Roberto started the car. "Where to—now?"

"I know just the place to lift my spirits. The town square has a wonderful toy store."

Roberto shook his head. "That baby is going to be so spoiled."

"Yes. That's my plan." Rose Ellen's mind bounced from worrying about her sister to losing her ring forever. She stared out the window as they made the quick drive to the square.

Once parked, they walked across the street past the Gold Museum. Roberto held open the door of the Giggle Monkey Toys store for Rose Ellen. A curvy middle-age blond greeted them, her eyes lingered on Roberto. "Hello. How can I help you?" Her southern drawl dripped with charm.

Rose Ellen smiled and tucked her arm around Roberto's, pulling him close. "We're looking for a baby gift for my first grandchild."

The woman diverted her attention to Rose Ellen and extended a hand towards a display in the back of the store. "We've got a lovely selection of infant toys over here." She walked ahead, swaying her hips—

much like the way Rose Ellen had done the first day she'd met Roberto. *Save it for someone else. He's mine.*

As they passed a shelf of stuffed animals, Rose Ellen lingered looking at a plush rabbit, and rubbing its long silky ear. Roberto picked up a pink squishy ball and bobbled it from one hand to the other. He raised his brows and grinned.

"Cute, dear. But not appropriate for a newborn."

He winked and placed it back on the shelf. "I wasn't thinking about the baby. It reminded me of something else."

Rose Ellen laughed and whispered in his ear. "You're so bad."

He patted her on the rear. "Bel fiore, you knew that when you met me."

Chapter Twenty-Eight

When Chuck hadn't returned to the house Monday night, Sam became concerned. The grown man didn't need to report to him, but it seemed unlikely he would leave without saying a word. They'd formed a respectful relationship since he'd been staying with him and Mutzi.

Curiosity and worry made for a restless night's sleep. Tuesday morning Sam decided to drive into town, swinging by the gold mine to see if Chuck had shown up for work. The blue sedan sat in the empty parking lot. He decided to park and go inside.

When he reached the door, he noticed the small "closed until further notice" sign taped to it. A nauseous feeling stirred in his belly. *Why would Chuck's car still be here if they'd closed?*

He got back in the car and headed into the town square, parking near the barber shop, hoping someone there would tell him why the mine closed. As he walked across the street, Joe, the bartender at Shenanigan's Irish Pub, came out, sporting a fresh crewcut.

"Surprised to see you here, Sam. Damn shame about that guy staying with you. Can't trust anybody now a days."

Sam stared at him. "Chuck? What are you talking about?"

Joe squinted in the strong sunlight, frown lines forming on his broad forehead. "Haven't you heard what happened?"

"Apparently not."

"Found him trying to rape a young college chick. The mine collapsed on both of them. A crew dug them out and took them to the hospital." He shook his head. "Damn shame it didn't kill the creep."

The news punched Sam in the gut, taking his breath, and making his pulse quicken. "That's a defaming accusation, Joe. It doesn't sound like something Chuck would do." Sam wiped sweat from his brow. "You sure you got the facts and not just some local gossip?"

"Word's spreading around town like syrup on a hot pancake. Someone said he was staying with you. Couldn't believe you'd take in a guy like that. Did you know he spent time in prison for the same type of offense?" Joe folded his arms against his chest and frowned. "Don't know why they let those kind out. They should just shoot guys who do that. No trial. Nothing."

"That's not the whole story." Sam released an exasperated sigh. "I don't have time to explain, but please—stop. It's not true. The guy's been through enough. There's got to be more to this story. Give him a chance to tell his side."

"Not much for him to tell. Domenic says he had the hots for the girl and they found him half naked on top of her." Joe put his hands on his hips. "There are evil people in this world, Sam. Not all of them are good guys like you."

"Not all of them bad, either." Sam dug the keys from his pocket. "I've gotta go."

The fifteen minute drive back to the house provided Sam time to decide what he'd say to Mutzi. It wasn't his place to tell Chuck's story, but she needed to know before the town gossip reached her.

As he crossed the creek going up his driveway, he saw her sitting on the front porch. She stood and walked down the steps meeting him when he parked the truck.

Sam took her hand and gave her a peck on the cheek. "We need to talk."

Mutzi nodded and led the way to the bench under the tall oak. "There's a nice breeze over here. Good for talking."

The unusually calm response surprised Sam. Still, what he had to tell her wouldn't be easy. He waited for her to sit and then started to pace. The irony of the reverse roles would have made him laugh if the situation wasn't so serious.

"There's been a collapse at the gold mine. Chuck and Brandi were injured."

Mutzi nodded, seemingly not rattled by the news. "Marge already called. The hospital is trying to get hold of Brandi's parents. She's beside herself with worry." Mutzi squeezed Sam's hand. "Rose Ellen called, too. Wanted to warn me about Chuck's past. Ten minutes later, Thelma called to fill me in on the rest."

Sam closed his eyes for a moment, then touched Mutzi's hand. "I should have told you sooner. I'm sorry."

"Wasn't yours to tell." Mutzi took a deep breath. "Fact is, Chuck told me everything the day I yelled at him. We took a walk and we both shared a lot of things."

The words surprised and comforted Sam. He knew they'd talked, but had no idea what brought about the change in Mutzi's attitude toward Chuck.

"You know he didn't do it—didn't rape and murder that girl he went to prison for?"

"Yup." She pressed her lips tight. "Mark my word. He didn't hurt Brandi either."

Sam stared into Mutzi's eyes. "I can't believe you knew and didn't say anything."

"Not much to say."

Sam stood. "We should drive to the hospital and check on them."

Mutzi remained seated and took Sam's hand again. "Not yet. We're not done talking."

He eased back down onto the bench, anxious to hear what else she had to say.

"When you invited Chuck to stay here, I freaked out." Mutzi rubbed her legs and rocked. "I never told you why, but I told Chuck. It's time you know, too."

Sam blinked and tried to clear his head. His wife shared a secret with a stranger before telling him. The realization unsettled him. "I'm listening."

"After you left for Vietnam, Marge got married and went on her honeymoon. I lived in Daddy's house for a little while by myself." Mutzi squirmed on the bench. "One day this guy came by and started talking to me. We sat on the porch for a while. I asked him if he knew you and he said he did." She drew in a breath and released it with her eyes closed. "I should have known he was lying, but I was so excited to talk to someone about you."

Mutzi stood with her back to Sam. "He asked to use the bathroom so I let him in the house."

Sam rose from the bench, sensing whatever she was going to say wasn't good. He moved next to her, choosing not to interrupt.

"I was so naïve." Her voice broke. "I never knew what evil things a man could do. He hurt me—really bad."

"Oh, Mutzi. My love." Sam inched closer, wanting to wrap his arm around Mutzi and hold her tight.

She flinched and stepped back.

"The blood—it was everywhere. I tried to stop it—but it kept getting worse. And the pain. I couldn't take the pain. I thought I would die. So I went to the hospital. They could tell I'd been raped, even though I denied it."

"I'm so sorry." He opened her arms and offered to hold her. She didn't resist. Instead, she buried her head in his chest and wept. Sam allowed his own tears to flow as her body shuddered. When she released her grip around his waist, he reached into his pocket and pulled out a handkerchief for her.

"I let him in my house. I should have known better." Her voice trembled as she spoke. "I blamed myself...for a long time. And the worse part..." A sob choked her words. "They said I'd never be able to have children, and I knew how much you wanted a family. I hated myself."

The painful admission broke through his defense and the tears flowed again. All these years they'd both suffered the pains of knowing they couldn't fulfill the other one's dreams. How cruel life could be at times.

Sam shook his head, unable to find the words to describe the hole it tore in his heart. Unfamiliar rage boiled in his gut. The need to destroy the man who did this to her grew, yet his years of training and counseling others, wrestled with the urge. Anger and hatred served no purpose. Yet, he wanted—needed, some kind of assurance the man paid for his actions.

"Did they find him? Charge him?"

"No." She let him hold her for a while without speaking.

When she stepped away, she continued, "The shame of letting him into the house, combined with the guilt I carried about taking Rose Ellen's ring, consumed me. I think that's when all my crazy superstitions started. I couldn't stop them."

It all made sense now. Her hostile reaction to Chuck's unplanned visit, the fact she'd never dated or married when Sam didn't return. It even explained her hesitation in marrying him. She'd bore the pain all these years and it broke his heart.

"I moved in with Marge when they came back from their honeymoon. Told her I didn't want the responsibility of taking care of Daddy's house. I never told her the truth. Never told anyone." She took a tissue from her smock and blew her nose. "Never let another man touch me, not that any tried. I felt safe with Marge. I felt safe with you, until you brought Chuck here."

He winced. "I wouldn't have brought him here had I known, honey." He wiped a tear trickling down her face. "No more secrets. Okay?"

"No more surprise guests." Mutzi chuckled as she took another tissue out of her smock and wiped his tear-stained face.

Sam lifted Mutzi's chin and touched his lips to hers. "No more surprise guests. Promise."

"Unless it's another dog. I can handle four legged guests."

He laughed. "Let's go check on Chuck and Brandi. I'm sure Marge could use some support by now."

"Chuck could use some too." She looked up at Sam. "How are we going to help him get out of this mess?"

"Been praying about that already. We'll find a way."

Chapter Twenty-Nine

Thanks to the incomplete report furnished to the police, guards monitored Chuck's hospital room twenty-four seven. In appreciation of the help, the rookie cop promised to keep Domenic informed. An arrest warrant awaited Chuck as soon as doctors allowed them to issue it.

Domenic reasoned the guy did time for someone else's crime before, wasting most of his life in jail, he could do it again. What's a few more years?

The prognosis for Brandi concerned Domenic. She might remain in a coma for some time, based on the swelling in her brain from the blow to her head. He could visit her and pretend to be the grieving boyfriend, but what if she woke and remembered. Domenic decided his best bet would be to disappear once they'd arrested Chuck. He'd already secured enough gold from the jewelry he'd stolen to last a year. All he needed to do was be patient, not one of the things he did well, as the red-head learned the hard way.

After wearing a path in the carpet of his living room, Domenic grabbed his keys and drove to the hospital, unsure exactly what he'd do when he got there, but staying locked up in his condo wasn't working.

"That's—not—what happened." Chuck winced from back spasms that continued to stab relentlessly. Pressing the morphine pump attached to him seemed to offer little help. His lungs burned as his halted words fell on deaf ears.

The smug young officer continued to push him for a confession. "I get it, man. She's a beautiful young thing." He nodded and folded his arms. "Just admit it. You'll never convince a jury you didn't do it. Look how they found you. Besides, your fingerprints were all over that paperweight." He turned and walked toward the door.

Chuck writhed another denial. "I—didn't hurt her."

"That's what all the sickos say."

It was déjà vu. Chuck closed his eyes and prayed to a god he'd just begun to trust again. *I can't go through this again. Please let Brandi live.* Exhaustion overcame him and his body finally gave into the drugs and sleep.

The disturbing dream wormed through his slumber. Inside the ominous courtroom, the judge who presided over his first trial, sat on the bench. Domenic, dressed in suit and tie, testified from the witness stand, smirking at Chuck as each lie flowed from his mouth. The jurors stood together and yelled as one, "Guilty," as the judge's oversized mallet slammed the table.

Chuck's body lurched, waking him with a muffled scream to find Domenic standing next to his bed. Unsure if it was still a dream, he closed his eyes again. When he opened them, the evil man stood staring at him with the same disgusting smirk.

"Have to thank you, Chuck. You showed up right on schedule. Couldn't have made a better alibi for myself if I tried."

"What—are you—doing in here?" Chuck gasped between words, struggling to free his arms and legs in an effort to jump up and strangle the man. The shackles on his wrist prevented him from even taking a swing.

"I gave your guard a coffee break. Nice fellow. Little naïve, but that works to my benefit."

Each breath tore at Chuck's lungs, making them burn more. "You bastard. How—could you do that? How could you—leave her to die?"

Domenic shrugged his shoulders. "Terrible accident." He squinted his eyes, pure wickedness oozing from his glare. "The tramp should have died. You screwed that up. Now you'll pay for it."

The man drew closer. Chuck's fingers searched the bed for the call button, unable to reach it. Domenic lifted it and laughed. "Is this what you want?" He dropped it alongside the bed, turned, and walked away.

"By the way, they found some stolen jewelry in your locker. Shame on you." As he walked out, he high-fived the officer who'd just returned.

Chapter Thirty

The ventilator hissed as it forced air into Brandi's lungs. Doctors assured Marge the best option to allow her brain to heal was a medically induced coma. They'd warned her surgery might be necessary if the swelling continued. Although Marge had medical authority to act on behalf of the triplets, she didn't want to be forced to make such a serious decision.

The urgent message she'd left for her parents had gone unanswered. Ashley had spent the night at Brandi's side, but when Marge arrived, she'd convinced her to go back to the house for a shower and some sleep. Chelsea had left for London the week after she broke the news to her sisters. Although she wanted to be there for her sister, she didn't want to lose the internship she'd worked so hard to receive. If Brandi's condition worsened, she'd return, but until then, she promised to keep in close touch.

Bandages hid most of the young woman's soft red hair, but a few wisps of it trailed her neckline. Marge touched the locks, appeasing her strong urge to cradle the injured child in her arms. Scrapes and purple blotches covered her exposed arms and neck. She could only imagine the pain the rest of her body bore.

As Marge sat in the chair next to Brandi, the last few unsettling days swirled in her mind. Learning the results of the ancestry test had consumed her thoughts—until hearing from Rose Ellen about Chuck's past. Then, she fretted about Mutzi's safety.

The horrific accident at the gold mine delivered another, even heavier blow. Brandi unconscious, Chuck injured. While she wasn't keen on his past, she wished him no harm.

As if that wasn't enough to worry about, the conversation she wasn't meant to hear frightened her even more. The hard, stern glare the creepy man directed toward her as they'd passed in the hall had made the hair on her neck stand up, and a quiver snake up her spine.

Unwilling to ignore the seriousness of the situation, Marge took out a notepad from her Gucci leather mini bag and started writing, her heart palpitating with each chosen word. She closed her eyes and struggled to capture each detail, not wanting to rely later on her aging memory.

Fifteen minutes passed before a nurse came to check on Brandi. The stout woman adjusted the drip on the IV and entered something into the nearby laptop. Apparently, paper charts were a thing of the past. Marge watched in silence as the woman checked her vitals.

As the nurse walked toward the door, she said, "There are two visitors waiting to see Ms. McDougal."

"Of course. I'll step out." Marge tucked her pen and paper into her handbag and walked to the waiting room in hopes of finding Brandi's parents. Instead, she saw Mutzi. The yellow polka dot smock and purple stripes leggings made her smile. Sam dropped the magazine he was reading and jumped up when Marge came in.

"How's she doing?" He stepped closer to Marge, his eyes filled with concern.

The need to hold onto someone overcame Marge and she wrapped her arms around Sam and began sobbing. All the weight on her shoulders poured out in tears. When she finished, she released her hold and stepped back, taking a hanky from her pocket and wiping her face. "I'm sorry. I—don't know what came over me."

Mutzi's eyes bulged. "Is she dead?"

"No. No." Marge realized she'd frightened her sister. Her normal role as a strong, self-controlled woman failed her today. She drew in a deep breath and released it.

"They've put her in a coma to help the healing process. Her vitals are good, but they don't know if there will be any permanent damage until they bring her out of the coma."

Sam took hold of Marge's arm and led her to the chair next to where her sister stood. "What about you? Are you okay? I'm concerned."

She sat down and forced a smile. "I'll be fine. I'm sorry. That was inappropriate."

"Don't be silly. It's an emotional time. Sometimes a body needs a good cry."

Mutzi stood in front of Marge, a frown drawing her brows tight. "You don't ever fall apart. What else is going on?"

With her elbows on her purse, Marge held her face in her palms. She didn't have the energy to explain everything now, but she needed to say something. "The gold mine accident, Brandi's injuries. Not being able to reach her parents." She refused to look at her sister, their bond so close she knew Mutzi would read more into her eyes.

"You should go in and see Brandi."

Mutzi didn't move. "What else is going on?"

"Isn't that enough?" Marge closed her eyes, emotionally drained. "Rose Ellen called me about something she heard."

Mutzi's face firmed. "It was about Chuck, wasn't it?" She pursed her lips, arms folded tight against her chest. "People need to mind their own damn business. He didn't hurt that girl."

Her sister's strong reaction surprised Marge. She hadn't expected her to defend him. "I don't know what to believe. I'm worried about him staying with you."

Sam spoke up. "Chuck spent time in prison for a crime he didn't commit. Unfortunately, his past upsets people who don't know the whole story. He told me everything when I first met and offered him refuge. Believe me, I'd never put your sister in danger."

The reassurance eased Marge's mind a little. "They've had a guard outside his door."

"They won't let us see him and won't tell us his condition." Sam shook his head. "I can't imagine what he's going through. I'm not sure how we can help him, but someone needs to."

The words settled into Marge's mind. She took Mutzi's hand. "I need to take care of some things. Will you stay with Brandi until I get back, or at least until Ashley returns?"

Mutzi nodded. "I'll stay." She turned to Sam. "Maybe you could go see Father Mitch and ask him to come by to see Brandi. They might let him talk with Chuck, too."

"That's a good idea." He kissed Mutzi and motioned to Marge. "Come on, we'll walk out together."

Marge followed him into the hall.

As they approached a restroom, Sam spoke. "I need to stop in here for a second. Mind waiting?

"No. Go ahead."

Marge wandered down the hall to where the guard stood outside Chuck's room. The door was ajar, so Marge stopped, pretending to look for something in her purse. She strained to listen as the nurse asked Chuck for his birthdate—a coughing spell followed his raspy reply.

Sam walked down the hall toward her and tried to get a glance of him before the nurse pulled the door close. When he met up with Marge, he inquired, "Did you get a look at Chuck?"

"No. But, he's awake. Couldn't see his face, but I heard him respond. The nurse was giving him some meds."

"Poor guy's been through so much. Can't catch a break." He sighed. "Sure could use a guardian angel."

Chuck definitely needed someone to intervene, angel or not. She wasn't sure how much she could help, but she was willing to try.

Chapter Thirty-One

You have the right to remain silent. Anything you say or do can and will be used against you in a court of law. You have the right to an attorney."

Like I could afford one of those. The words settled in Chuck's mind as the deputy rattled on. He'd anticipated the arrest since Domenic's visit. Pure evil, that man. He recognized it the first day in the way he leered at Brandi. It made Chuck's stomach churn. The disrespectful manner he treated his uncle disgusted him too, but he hadn't anticipated the man could sink so low as to rape a young woman and leave her to die.

The nurse asked the deputy to step out of the room as she removed the IV port from his battered and bruised arm.

The officer glared from her to Chuck. "Don't get any crazy ideas. I'm going to be right outside." He patted the holstered gun hanging from his waist.

The nurse tossed a set of scrubs to Chuck. "You'll have to wear these. The cops took all your clothes."

"Thanks. I appreciate all the staff. Please, let them know." The few days of physical therapy and meds helped ease the unbearable back pain. Nurses spoke kindly to him, and even the cleaning men and women were jovial.

The nurse tilted her head and paused. "Not sure what happened with you, but you don't seem like a bad guy."

"I'm not. Wrong place, wrong time."

He nodded and slipped the baggy pants on underneath his gown. When she left the room to get the paperwork for his discharge, he finished dressing. He looked down at the grey, skid-free slippers on his feet and shook his head. "Even took my damn shoes and socks."

The restless deputy stepped back into the room and paced the tile floor. "What's taking so long?"

"They're doing their job. What's the big hurry?"

"Bet you'd like to stay here. Probably feels like a Holiday Inn to a homeless guy."

The man spoke the truth. Chuck was grateful for the meals and respectfulness. He'd taken nothing for granted, appreciating the tree-filled atrium outside his window, the powder blue privacy curtain that surrounded his power lift bed, and even the clean, antiseptic scents others often complained about smelling.

The deputy walked closer to Chuck, a nasty sneer inched across his face.

The click of the handcuffs spiraled Chuck's spirit to darkness. *How could this have happened—again?* Sam helped restore his dreams of reentering the work force, saving enough to get his own place, having people who cared in his life. Hope disintegrated like the morning mist rising from the valley.

As he climbed into the cruiser, bile rose in his throat. He'd rather die than go back to another depressing gray cube that reeked of urine and feces, with roaches and mice having more freedom than the inmates. No family, friends to visit him. The frustration of not being able to prove his innocence pierced his soul like the blade of a knife.

Chapter Thirty-Two

Marge stood by Brandi's bed and stared at the still comatose girl. Grateful her vitals were stable enough to move her from the ICU into a step-down unit, Marge closed her eyes and offered a prayer of thanks. The three excruciating days she'd waited for her parents to respond to her message drained her energy. It took another two days before they could get a flight out from London where they had gone to help Chelsea get settled into her new surroundings. Marge expected them to arrive soon.

Within the hour, Celeste McDougal walked into the room, pausing just a foot inside the door as if she might be intruding.

Marge walked over to her and greeted her. "I'm so glad you made it."

"Thank you for staying with Brandi until we could get here."

Marge moved toward the bed, glancing toward the young woman. "She's been resting peacefully. The doctor's may try to wake her today."

Celeste nodded in silence but didn't move. The cool, distant reaction confused Marge. She'd expected a teary, emotional response from the woman who almost lost her daughter. The stoic, hardened face made the room feel cold. Marge pulled the covers up around Brandi.

Evan McDougal strolled in and walked straight to the window, as if his daughter, nor anyone else was in the room. "Terrible reception," he muttered while stabbing the phone with his manicured finger. His furrowed brows creased his forehead as he turned and looked up toward the bed for a second, still tapping at the phone. "There's no reception in here. I'm going outside."

The man turned and stormed past his wife without as much as a nod. Celeste remained frozen in place, a mere six inches inside the doorway. Marge frowned, disappointed in the lack of compassion from either parent. *Such a strange couple.*

The conversation Ashley had with Marge the night of their dinner stirred from the recesses of her mind. Could this couple be as callous as the girl implied? It broke her heart to think she might be right. Still, she refused to believe they didn't care. Perhaps they were exhausted from the trip or maybe, like Marge, they had other heavy issues weighing on their minds.

"Would you like to sit by the bed and talk to her alone?"

The woman's eyes widened. "Talk to her? Why? She's in a coma."

"Doctors believe patients can hear, even though they might not be able to respond."

Celeste took a few steps closer and lingered near the chair Marge had moved close to the bed. "I—I don't know what I'd say. I've never been very good at this sort of thing."

"Maybe you could start with saying her name and telling her you're here. I've told her you were coming."

"All the bruising. Her face. It doesn't even look like my daughter." Celeste's eyes glistened with unshed tears.

"It's difficult to see her like this. I was shocked too. But she's alive and improving every day, little by little. I know she's going to be so happy to see you."

Celeste lifted her eyes to meet Marge's. "Do you think so? I'm not sure."

"Of course she will. You're her mother, and she loves you."

"I haven't been a very good mother to her...to any of them. I let other women raise them while I focused on our family's business." Her voice broke. "We've never been close." She brushed away a tear. "She could have died not knowing how much I love her."

"But she didn't. It's not too late. You've been given another chance."

Celeste nodded.

Marge picked up her purse and took out some tissue, handing it to Celeste. "I'm going to grab some coffee. Can I get you something?"

"Thank you. A cappuccino would be nice." Celeste eased into the chair and reached a trembling hand close enough to stroke Brandi's cheek.

The simple gesture reassured Marge as she left the room. By the time she reached the hall, she heard the woman whisper to her daughter.

"Hello, Brandi. It's Mom. I'm here now. I love you, honey."

Marge's heart swelled and she smiled to herself. *Every cloud has a silver lining.*

The brief uplifting moment faded when she passed Chuck's empty hospital room. She was disappointed her talk with the sheriff failed to prevent his arrest. The officer's words still lingered in her mind. "We've been friends a long time, Marge. You know I can't act on hearsay. Bring me some solid evidence, and I'll look into it."

It was time for her to implement plan B. She dug out her phone and dialed as she made her way to the cafeteria. By the time she'd paid for their coffees and returned, all the calls were made. Time for the family to unite.

Bernie Trentworth took the arresting officer's advice and completed an inventory of the gold mine's jewelry collection. Including the pieces found in Chuck's locker, at least two dozen more were missing. He scribbled each item on a sheet of paper and estimated the value. The unaccounted for diamonds, gold chains, and precious stones totaled more than $500,000.

The turmoil of the past week weighed heavy on his shoulders. Shutting down the mine meant no income to pay for the outrageous cost of repairing the damages. As upsetting as that was, his foremost concern was the health of the two injured workers. There hadn't been a collapse at the mine during all the years he'd owned it. He couldn't understand how it had happened now.

He walked into the office with the paper clutched in his hand, intending to report his findings to the police and insurance company. When he sat down, his knee bumped the safe tucked from sight under the large oak desk. The familiar jolt triggered another thought. The ring he'd found in the cave needed to be returned to its rightful owner. He didn't know how it got there, but he knew who it belonged to, even remembered when the jeweler who made it was commissioned to design it years ago.

There'd been a big fuss over the unique ring last year. Someone started a rumor it had been stolen from the Gold Museum. It proved to be a bunch of old lady gossip. He knew better, but gossip had a way of spreading in small towns. He reached down to unlock the safe and the unsecured door opened.

"What the hell?" The shock sent him to his knees. He peered inside the empty box. Everything was gone. The emergency cash he'd kept on hand, the rare Rolex watch his father had left him when he passed, even the gold miner's ring, nowhere in sight. An angry scream tore through his throat and echoed throughout the massive building.

Chapter Thirty-Three

The impromptu mid-week dinner invite surprised Mutzi. She and Sam arrived as April and Paul climbed the steps of the large Victorian house. April paused when they got to the top step and stretched her back. Mutzi turned toward her and patted her slightly protruding midsection. "Too much the ice cream?"

April elbowed Mutzi. "I am not fat! That's all baby."

Mutzi roared with laughter. "Just teasing you. You look great. How are you feeling?'

"I'm fine. No morning sickness or anything."

"That's good." Feeling feisty, Mutzi turned to Paul and winked. "Hey, did you know eating bananas helps the chances of it being a boy?" She shot a glance at April knowing the suggestion would make her fume.

Paul played along and wrapped an arm around April. "Honey, I think we'll have to stop at the grocery store on the way home."

April gave Mutzi an evil eye as she squirmed away from Paul. "Don't bother. I won't eat another banana the rest of my pregnancy."

"It's just an old wives tale, but maybe Marge would make you a banana pie or two." Mutzi laughed and hurried toward the front door.

April shook her head. "You and your crazy superstitions. By the way, what's this family meeting about?"

Mutzi shrugged, then chuckled. "Darned if I know. I came for the food."

Sam held the front door open and waited for the other three to enter.

Rose Ellen called out from the dining room. "Roberto and I are in here."

Mutzi led the wave of family following Rose Ellen's voice. "Hey, sis, Roberto."

"Good to see you." Rose Ellen and Roberto responded as one.

April gave her mom a hug and took a seat next to her. "Where's Aunt Marge?"

"She's doing something on the computer. Told me to open a bottle of wine and she'd be done in a five minutes." Rose Ellen rolled her eyes. "That was ten minutes ago."

A delectable aroma of garlic, oregano, and basil drew Mutzi to the kitchen. "Meatballs and spaghetti. Yum." She snatched a slice from the French loaf on the counter and went looking for her sister.

Marge greeted her on her third step down the hall. "I'm coming." She eyed the cheese bread in Mutzi's hand. "Some things don't change." She laughed and gave her a hug. "How you doing, Sis?"

"Crazy week, but I guess you know that better than any of us. How are you holding up?"

"Better, now that Brandi is off the ventilator and her parents are here. She's awake, but having trouble remembering things. I'm more worried about Chuck and his situation."

Mutzi watched Marge's eyes brim with moisture as she shook her head. "Do you think she'll be able to clear him?"

"I'm sorry. I can't seem to talk about it without crying." She took out a tissue and wiped away the spilled tears and then hurried into the dining room.

Mutzi followed and took a seat at the table.

"Hello, everyone. Thank you for coming." Marge removed a wad of papers from her apron pocket and slipped them into a linen drawer. "Dinner's almost ready. I thought we'd eat cafeteria style. The plates are in the kitchen."

She turned to April and Paul. "Why don't you two get us started?"

April jumped to her feet. "Don't have to ask me twice. I'm eating for two."

Rose Ellen's bottom lip protruded into a ridiculous pout. "I thought we were still considered guests."

Sometimes her older sister's need for attention exceeded Marge's patience, so she chose to ignore the comment. "How about pouring me a glass of wine?" She needed a little fortification to get through the next few hours.

With an exaggerated sigh, Rose Ellen lifted the decanter and poured the red liquid, handing it to her sister. "When are you going to tell us about this family meeting?"

Marge's face twitched. "After we enjoy our dessert."

"I hate waiting."

A loud chuckle erupted from April. "You didn't have to tell us that. We all know it."

Once everyone had their plates piled high and was seated, Marge led them in prayer. After giving thanks for the usual food and family, she added, "Lord, nourish our hearts and minds and guide us to help those most in need."

The clink of forks on the china plates replaced the table chatter as everyone consumed the fare. Marge poked at her salad, taking small bites and thinking about the discussion they'd have later. Nerves diminished her appetite, but fortunately, not that of her guests.

"Perfecto. Fresh Parmesan cheese and creamy Caesar dressing." Roberto closed his eyes as if savoring the mouth full. "The salad is exquisite."

Marge smiled. "Thanks."

"She makes the best food in town." Mutzi reached across the table for another chunk of bread.

"Best I've ever tasted." Sam nodded as he used a slice of bread to gather the last dab of sauce from his plate.

Seeing all the nearly empty dishes pleased Marge. "There's plenty more for seconds. Help yourself."

"Not me. I'm saving room for that chocolate cake." Mutzi stood and started collecting empty plates.

Paul held onto his when Mutzi tried to take it. "I'm going for seconds."

Sam nodded. "Me, too."

Rose Ellen folded her arms across her chest. "Well, I'm ready for cake. Don't see why we need to wait on the men."

"I agree." Mutzi took the empty dishes to the kitchen and returned with the cake.

Marge shook her head as she stood and moved to the china cabinet. "I'm glad you're enjoying the meal." She pulled out a stack of dessert plates and set them on the table. "By the way, how is...Shadow? I think that's his name."

The question brought a huge grin to Mutzi's face. "Yep. Shadow. I was a little concerned because he stopped eating for a day or two when Chuck didn't come home." She picked up a serving knife and sliced some cake. "He's a smart one. I've been teaching him some tricks."

With fork in hand, Rose Ellen waited for Mutzi to serve her a slice. Instead, she handed the plate to Marge.

Rose Ellen reached across the table and grabbed the knife from Mutzi to cut a piece for herself. "Would you like a slice, April?"

"Sure." April grinned as she met Mutzi's eyes and then reached and took the one Rose Ellen cut.

The wide-eyed glare from Rose Ellen said it all. "For heaven's sake. Such rudeness."

Mutzi chuckled. "Don't be such a bad sport, sis. We're just messing with you."

Marge looked away, stifling a giggle at the silliness. "I'll get the coffee." She walked to the kitchen and returned with a carafe, being sure to pour Rose Ellen's first.

The men had returned from the kitchen and consumed their second round of pasta and salad before Marge had a chance to sit down.

Paul nudged April and smiled. "Maybe you could get some of your aunt's recipes."

"What are you saying, my cooking isn't as good?" April threw her napkin down and folded her arms across her chest, pouting like a child.

Mutzi intervened. "Come on, April. Give Paul a break. Admit it. Nobody cooks as well as Marge.

April sighed and nodded. "You're right." She glanced at Paul. "But you'll be doing all the cooking next week as punishment." She laughed as she slid another piece of cake into her mouth.

Rose Ellen licked her fork to retrieve the last smear of chocolate from it. "This is scrumptious, Marge."

"Thanks."

Mutzi sliced some cake and handed it to Sam and Paul. "Are you ready for a piece, Roberto?"

"Ah, yes. Please."

Rose Ellen placed her napkin on the empty plate. "I'm ready to hear about this family meeting."

Marge turned in her chair and pulled open the linen drawer, removed the stack of papers, and placed them on the table, resting her hands on top of them. "Let's talk."

Chapter Thirty-Four

Exhaustion sent Chuck into a deep, restless slumber. The same dream which haunted him for years replayed the dreadful night that changed his life forever.

The dark moonless night cast a heaviness accentuating the acrid scent coming from the nearby alley. Chuck nodded from the stoop outside his motel, as the sociable young neighbor waved to him as she turned into the alley and headed to her place. He watched as she disappeared from sight, then finished the last drag of his cigarette and stomped it out.

A movement caught his attention. A scraggly-haired man staggered in the same direction, sucking the last drop of beer from a can and tossing it to the oil-stained curb. The pitiful drunk made Chuck thankful he'd given up his heavy drinking habit. *What a wasteful life.*

Once in his room, Chuck decided he'd take a shower and crash for the night. He slipped off his jeans and walked to the door to be sure it was locked. A blood-curdling scream came from the backstreet.

He remembered the drunk. Fear for whomever continued to scream sent him charging into the darkness in his bare feet and unclothed body.

He squinted, trying to locate the source of the excruciating cry for help he'd heard. The silence confused him. Not even a mere whimper echoed through the silent pathway. He inched closer to the filthy dumpster gasping when he saw the woman's crumpled body, her throat slit from ear to ear. He bent down and tried in vain to stop the flow of blood. Sirens wailed in the distance.

A clinking sound disrupted the painful dream and Chuck's eyes flew open.

"Let's go, Hansen" The prison warden slipped a key into the cell's cage. The hefty, balding man checked his watch as he waited.

Chuck rubbed his eyes trying to erase the nightmare. With a groan, he pushed up from the low, hard bunk, pressing a hand on the rough concrete wall for balance until he could stand upright. "Where are we going?"

"I'm not going anywhere. You're leaving."

The words sunk into the pit of Chuck's stomach. As far as his experience in jails, the clean Lumpkin County Jail didn't seem too bad. "Where are they sending me?"

The warden stared at him and shook his head. "You're free to go, but you have to stay in Dahlonega until your trial date."

Chuck stroked his week-old beard as he followed behind the warden. "I don't understand. At the hearing, the judge said no bail."

When the warden neared his desk, he picked up a pen and signed a log. "Don't know what to tell you. Guess he changed his mind."

The man lectured Chuck about the restrictions of his release. Most of what he said blurred into garbled chatter as Chuck tried to understand what was happening. Something wasn't right. Maybe Brandi came out of the coma and cleared him. But wouldn't the charges have been dropped? With a punch to his gut, another possibility came to mind.

Was this a set up? The years he'd spent behind bars taught him not to trust unexplained good news. He remembered a guy who claimed his innocence, said he'd witnessed someone else commit a murder. When a glitch in the system granted him an unexpected release, he met with death before the sun set.

The lowlife, Domenic, was willing to let a young woman die. If the creep would let Brandi die, he wouldn't hesitate to take him out too. Chuck rubbed his neck and the muscles in his jaw tightened as he contemplated his options. Where would he go? He couldn't go back to Sam's. Wouldn't put him or Mutzi at risk. Only other choice he had was his car. It served him well for months before Sam offered refuge. He'd just have to thumb a ride or hike to the gold mine to get it.

"Hey, Hansen Did you get all that?" The warden scowled at him waiting for a response.

Chuck gazed at the pen the man handed him. "Don't leave town. Got it." He looked down at the papers, unable to clear his head of the fear creeping up his neck. "My keys. I need my keys."

The warden shook his head. "They didn't send anything when you were brought in." He shrugged. "Maybe the cops kept them or they were lost when you were in the hospital."

A headache pounded Chuck's skull like the boulders that had crashed onto his back in the mine. He staggered out the door into the blinding sunlight. When the door closed behind him, he covered his eyes with one of his hands and held onto the building with the other. Once he steadied himself, he spread a small gap between two fingers in order to allow a little light to filter through.

"Sun's brutal today."

Chuck's heart thumped in his chest and he jumped back, squinting to focus in the direction of the voice. "Sam?"

"Thought you could use a ride." Sam patted Chuck on the shoulder. "Let's go home and get you a shower and hot meal.

Still confused about the situation, Chuck stood firm. "Brandi. Is—did she pull through?"

"She's doing better. They released her to her parents who took her back to Atlanta."

The news lifted Chuck's spirit for a moment. "So, she told them what happened?"

"Not yet, my friend." Sam ran a hand through his hair. "She hasn't regained her memory—yet. They're hoping it will come back soon."

"Then why did they release me?" Chuck's mind traveled back to his suspicions about Domenic.

"I don't know the specifics. What's important is you're out." Sam turned and motioned for Chuck to follow him to his truck.

"I'm not going back to your place." The pain in his head returned. "Can you give me a lift to my car?"

Sam looked away. "Somebody torched your car. It's been towed to a junk yard."

The news sent Chuck to his knees. His spirit shattered like broken glass and he hung his head, letting the long-held tears flow in huge sobs.

"It's going to be okay, Chuck. It really is." He offered a hand to help him up. "Come on back to the house and we'll talk."

"The bastard's not going to stop until I'm dead. I won't put you and Mutzi at risk."

"You're not going to have to worry about Domenic. Soon as they find him, he's going to be put away for a long time."

"Find him?" Chuck's heart thumped in his chest.

"He disappeared after coming to see you. They are looking for him."

"How'd you know he came to see me?"

"Marge saw him. It's a long story. They'll find him, soon. I'm sure."

"Well, I can't prove anything. If Brandi doesn't remember, I'm going back to jail."

"You're going to have to trust me on this one." He placed a hand on Chuck's shoulder. "A lot's happened since the mine collapse. You've got a small army helping you."

"Who? No one knows me except you and Mutzi."

"When those Dahlonega sisters get behind a project, they can move mountains."

The words sprinkled a few rays of light into Chuck's barren soul.

Chapter Thirty-Five

It took a couple days for Chuck to readjust to being back at Sam and Mutzi's house. Shadow clung to him every waking moment, keeping his mind off the upcoming trial and Brandi's still unrestored memory. At night, the black fur ball wailed from his pen, keeping all of them awake. After the second night, Sam agreed to let the poor thing stay in Chuck's room.

The pain in Chuck's back improved with the comfortable bed and some much needed medications. His headache eased as his nerves settled down, especially when word came about Domenic's arrest. Mutzi and Sam didn't mention the mine collapse and he appreciated it. He needed a few days to recover before reliving the details of the dreadful day.

Tonight the family planned to gather for dinner and fill him in on the details of his release. It seemed odd to him, but it would be an opportunity to thank them for their efforts.

The Smith House Restaurant was just east of the town square. Based on the crowded parking lot,

Chuck sensed the historic southern-style venue was a popular place. Sam found a spot when someone pulled out to leave and parked the truck. Chuck unbuckled his seat belt, intending to hurry out of the back seat in time to open Mutzi's door.

The spry woman jumped out and yanked open Chuck's door, a devilish grin plastered on her face. "Beat ya."

He laughed. Somehow the simple gesture had become a game between the two of them. "You sure did. I'll get you when this back heals up."

When they entered the building, the hostess showed them to a massive long table that seated at least a dozen. Chuck eyed the room and noticed all the tables were similar. Sam had told him it was a family style dining room, but he hadn't realized what that meant. Within ten minutes, Marge, Rose Ellen, and Roberto wandered in followed by April and Paul.

Once their drink orders were taken, Sam asked for everyone's attention. "Rather than me trying to explain everything all of you did to get Chuck released, the women wanted to do it as a family." He glanced toward Marge. "The floor's all yours."

She nodded and stood. "Well, I guess this all started when you were in the ICU. I was going past your room toward Brandi's room. I thought it strange when the guard wasn't outside your door, since one had been there every other time I'd come by. The door was opened a little and I overheard someone talking." Marge paused and took a sip of water. "I'm embarrassed to say this, but I stopped, peeked in, and listened. I wanted to know if you were awake. That's when I heard—Domenic—confess to hurting Brandi—and blaming you for it."

Chuck lowered his eyes, remembering the frustration of listening to his rants and not being able to do a thing about it.

Marge placed a hand across her chest. "I didn't get away fast enough and he saw me when he came out of the room. Gave me a frightening look. Scared the daylights out of me."

"He's a dangerous man. I wouldn't want you to cross him."

"Well, I couldn't let him get away with it. So I contacted the County Sheriff. Went straight to the top." Marge's shoulders pressed back and she extended her hand toward the two sitting next to her. "Then I called April. She and Paul are very good attorneys, and I asked them for help." Marge sat down.

April glanced at Paul and then met Chuck's eyes. "We were hesitant to get involved. The way they found you in the mine, the jewelry in your locker, and your previous conviction didn't help your case. Domenic fed enough misinformation to a rookie cop to paint a pretty grim picture."

"Fortunately for you, Mutzi had your back." Paul spoke as he nodded toward Mutzi. "With the information she provided us about your false imprisonment and some of Domenic's previous shady deals Mutzi found online, along with Marge's information, we convinced the sheriff to look further at the evidence."

Mutzi shrugged her shoulders. "Computers have their benefits. I keep telling you folks. You can find out most anything about most anyone."

"When they found the jewelry Domenic stole, they found my ring!" Rose Ellen folded her hands together and pressed them to her lips, her eyes brimming as she looked at Chuck. "I didn't really think you stole it."

Chuck shook his head. "You asked me to hold it when I was standing next to you at the party. I stuck it in my pocket and forgot about it." He tilted his head, a quizzical look on his face. "So, how did Domenic get it?"

Rose Ellen fluttered her hand in the air, appearing excited to provide an answer. "I bumped into Bernie Trentworth at The Cool Collective Jewelry Store on the square." She turned to her fiancé and smiled. "Roberto took me on a shopping spree." She fingered a pair of diamond studs in her ear lobes. "Bernie found the ring in the mine, right before he found you and Brandi. He put it in his safe to give it back to me, but when it went missing, he started checking the local jewelers for it. Turns out his no-good nephew stole it along with a bunch of other jewelry."

Chuck tilted his head and his eyes lit as if a light bulb came on. "Now I remember. Something fell out of my pocket when I took out my handkerchief. I couldn't see it in the dark, my flashlight quit."

Paul spoke up, "Mr. Trentworth knew you couldn't have stolen it from the safe because it happened after the collapse in the mine. I credit him with getting you released. If he hadn't turned his nephew in, you might still be a suspect in the theft."

Chuck couldn't believe all that had gone on while he was in the hospital and locked up. He hung his head, giving a quiet thanks to a higher power for bringing these good folks into his life.

Rose Ellen pulled something from her purse and turned to Chuck. "I wanted to do something special for you. I've been blessed with wealth, a loving family, and the kindest, sexiest, silver-haired fox I've ever known." She gave a quick wink toward Roberto as her cheeks flushed. "It's darn well time for you to feel blessed, too." She handed him a fob.

He drew his brows tight and studied the weird looking item. "What is this?"

"The keys to your new pick up. You looked like a truck guy to me. I hope you like it."

Chuck's mouth opened but he struggled to speak. "I—I can't afford a new truck. Heck, I can't even afford the gas to put in it."

Mutzi stood and walked toward Chuck. "We've all pitched in and taken care of that." She handed him an envelope. "Gas and insurance for six months." She scrunched her face tight. "After that, you're on your own, buster. But I get to keep the dog." The belly laugh that followed made everyone join in.

Chuck held the envelope and fob in trembling hands. "This is too much. Who does this kind of thing for a homeless guy?"

In one voice, Mutzi, Marge, and Rose Ellen answered. "The Dahlonega Sisters."

Chuck drew in a deep breath and released it, shaking his head. "I've met a lot of people through the years. Some of them not so good. Met a few with hearts of gold." He looked from one sister to the next. "Until I met you three, I never knew anyone with veins of gold."

Mutzi shrugged. "Well, Dahlonega is the first gold rush town in the US. Bet you didn't know a guy named Parks, a distant relative of Sam, kicked up a big chunk of gold in his field and started all the chaos around here."

Rose Ellen chimed in. "They had a big festival, naming a king and queen. The queen was presented a very special ring, exactly like the one Daddy commissioned just for me."

Marge added, "The festival became a tradition we still celebrate today."

"Guess that makes sense. Thank you. Know that I appreciate everything you've done for me. You're all amazing." He took a handkerchief from his pocket and wiped his eyes.

"We know." Rose Ellen grinned.

Chapter Thirty-Six

Tables and chairs filled the tree-covered side yard of Sam and Mutzi's place. Bright yellow, green, and pink balloons were tied to chairs. Blue and orange streamers entwined through the trees waved in the gentle breeze. Chuck had never seen such a beautiful sight. The laughter and comradery filled his heart with joy.

Mutzi had told him it was a celebration of life party. Although he wasn't familiar with such a thing, he didn't ask too many questions. Any reason to have a party suited him. The sisters didn't know the date they'd chosen happened to be his birthday. He wasn't one to bring attention to himself, so he'd decided to keep it under wrap. Maybe he'd tell them after the party.

As Chuck helped direct parking of the dozens of cars which overflowed into the yard, Shadow clung to his side. He'd been a little concerned about the dog chasing after the cars, but the furry fellow never wandered too far. Everyone stopped to pet his partner, sharing kind words and best wishes. It still seemed strange to be accepted by people he barely knew. They all seemed to know his story even if he didn't know theirs.

The changes during the past month had astounded Chuck. Once the town folks knew the truth about what happened in his past and at the gold mine cave in, they stepped forward and helped him get his life back on track. Bernie insisted he return to work and help reopen the gold mine.

The collapse in the mine proved to be a blessing. The once inaccessible vein of gold now provided enough income for Bernie to pay back his loans and repair the damages to the mine.

The folks at the Smith House Restaurant offered Chuck a room at their inn in exchange for some maintenance work. He'd accepted the extra work, able to squeeze it in when he wasn't at the mine, but continued to live with Sam and Mutzi, at least until he could find his own place. Mutzi threatened to hold Shadow hostage if he didn't stay, saying she'd make good on her promise to keep the dog.

Whenever he went to town, people paid for his meals and coffee. It never ceased to amaze him. Such a far cry from the treatment he received before he met Sam.

Grateful to Sam and Mutzi for all their support, he'd made paying kindness forward his mission. He'd taught Mutzi how to drive, helped Sam build a shed for his riding mower, and did simple chores like mowing grass and repairing roofs for neighbors who now had become friends.

As he directed the white SUV into a space, he recognized Brandi's cropped red hair pressed against the unopened back window. When her father turned off the engine, she jumped out and approached Chuck. "What's shaking, bro?" The sassy young woman kept him guessing.

Tears threatened to spill from Chuck's eyes as he stood like a soldier on guard duty, afraid to move, still unsure of Brandi's condition. Knowing the trauma she'd been through, he feared her reaction to seeing him.

Brandi's face paled as she looked into Chuck's eyes. "Are you mad at me?"

The unexpected question made Chuck gasp. "Mad at you? Why in the world would I be?"

"Because I made your life a pure hell. I'm so sorry. I wish I could have told them what happened right away instead of making you suffer for that creep's actions."

She remembered. Chuck opened his arms, holding them out to offer a hug, salty tears streaming down his cheeks. She moved close and wrapped her arms around him, looking up at him with crystal blue eyes.

"You have nothing to be sorry about. I'm so happy you pulled through. I was so worried about you."

"Thank you. For everything. Bet you're happy they dropped all the charges against you. No trial. I wanted to be the one to tell you, but I didn't remember until recently."

He'd been relieved to put the nightmare behind him, but worrying about Brandi never remembering what happened weighed heavy on his mind. He released a heavy sigh. "It's okay. Things happen for a reason. And everything's worked out well."

"How's your back? Heard you took some pretty bad hits trying to protect me."

"I'm fine. How about you?"

"I'm a hundred percent." Her eyes glistened as she spoke. "I've decided to change colleges. Didn't want the extra attention to distract me." She rolled her eyes. "You know how people talk. I've registered for engineering school in the fall."

"That's amazing. You've got the brains. I'm sure you'll do well."

Brandi's father and mother had stood aside as they talked. When the two paused their conversation, Evan approached, extending his hand. "Thank you for saving our daughter. We owe you for all you did."

Chuck shook his head. "Just followed my instincts. Right place at the right time."

Celeste met his eyes. "You risked your life and went to jail for it. I'd say that's pretty significant."

Chuck shifted from one foot to the other, unsure what to say. "I'm glad it's over. Finally, over." He noticed Ashley playing with Shadow. "He likes you."

She rubbed the dog's ears as he danced around. "He's so cute."

"What are your plans for next semester, Ashley?"

She stood, a huge grin spread across her face. "I'm coming back and staying with Ms. Marge again. I can't wait. This is such a special town. I love it. Maybe I can come play with Shadow sometime."

"He'd like that. He's a regular ham when it comes to getting attention." Chuck paused, trying to remember about the triplets. "What about your other sister? There's three of you, right?"

"Chelsea decided to stay in London and attend art school."

"That's great." Shadow wiggled around Chuck's ankles, aching for his attention. He bent and rubbed his ears. The dog licked his hand in appreciation. "Why don't you folks go find something to drink? I'll catch up with you in a bit and we'll talk some more." Another car pulled up, waiting to be directed to a parking space. Seemed half of the town had come for the celebration.

When there was a lull in the arrivals, Chuck made his way back up the hill to the party. With each step, he tried to imagine what it would have been like to grow up with a large family. As an only child, and then an orphan after his mother committed suicide, the loneliness created a void he'd never been able to fill. Being part of this noisy, energetic clan was as close as he'd ever come to feeling part of a family.

Chuck had to smile when he saw the three sisters standing in a huddle. They wore matching leather jackets and fancy jeans. He wondered how they'd ever convinced Mutzi to give up her smocks and leggings. He was sure he'd hear the story later.

Marge motioned for him to come to her. "Are you enjoying the celebration?"

"Of course. It's amazing. You know how to throw a party. Music, food, lots of folks. Who could ask for anything more?"

"There is more. Sit here for a minute." She stood next to his chair, waiting for something.

Chuck did as instructed, wondering what was going to happen next. "Shadow, sit." The dog settled down, leaning his head on Chuck's shoe.

Sam approached with a microphone and handed it to Marge.

"May I have—" The speaker screeched and Marge jumped. She tried again. "May I have your attention, please? Find a seat and we'll get started." She waited for the crowd to silence. "Thank you all for coming to our celebration of life. I'm sure some of you wondered exactly what that means. I'd like to tell you a story. It's rather long, so please bear with me. I think you'll find it worth the wait.

"Some months ago, I was contacted by a woman I didn't know. Her story was so bizarre, it frightened me. I was sure it wasn't true, but if it was, it would change our family dynamics." Marge looked at her sisters. "I liked our family just the way it was. I didn't want it to change." She pressed a hand to the side of her head when a gust of wind tousled her hair.

"I prayed about it, even spoke to Reverend Mitch for guidance. It took a young woman, Ashley McDougal, to make me realize that fearing the truth doesn't make it go away." She paused and picked up a glass of water, taking a sip.

"Now stay with me. This gets a little confusing." She looked toward Mutzi. "Some of you may be familiar with doing an ancestry DNA test. I don't understand all the genetic mapping part, but if you spit in this little tube and send it off, they send you a list of your relatives."

She looked to her left, locking eyes with Mutzi. "You didn't want me to dig into the past. I couldn't understand why, at least not until later."

Chuck watched as Mutzi continued to stare at Marge, barely blinking as she listened. He tried to imagine what was going through her mind. He remembered when he was in prison the advocacy group convinced him to take the test. Even though he knew his innocence, the fear of this still new scientific option unsettled him. What if it made things worse?

Marge cleared her throat and continued. "For years people questioned how we could be twins. We may not look anything alike, but I never doubted our relationship for a moment. And it didn't matter anyway. We are sisters at heart and nothing will change that. But, you were afraid the test would reveal to me we weren't."

Chuck leaned forward and watched the interaction between the twins. Mutzi swallowed hard as Marge continued.

"Imagine my surprise when I saw the results. That's when I realized, you'd already done the test."

Mutzi stood and looked as if she wanted to run. "Why are you doing this now? Why would you want to hurt me like this?"

Sam rose and put an arm around her shoulders, holding her close.

The furry and pain in her eyes made Chuck's heart ache.

Marge released a sigh and continued, "I wanted to do this now because the truth needs to be told. And it's not what you think."

Mutzi shook her head, tears streaming down her cheeks.

Marge went to Mutzi and gave her a hug. "Honey, we are sisters. Both our names are on the report. You didn't tell me you had already done the test. My name wasn't on yours because they can only track relatives who also have done a similar test." She smiled at her sister. "But we're not twins."

The revelation brought a number of gasps from the crowd. Mutzi's face twisted in confusion.

"Our mother gave birth to triplets. Two girls and a boy." Marge let the information hang in the air for a moment.

This time, Rose Ellen jumped to her feet. "That's wrong. I would have known if there was another child."

"Mother didn't even know. She was pretty sure she carried twins, but she didn't know there was a third baby."

Rose Ellen thrust her hands on her hips. "Then what happened to him?"

The restless crowd chattered among themselves. Marge took Mutzi's hand and walked back toward Chuck.

"Please, let me finish." Marge waited until the noise quieted. "The doctor's sister happened to give birth to a stillborn son the same day. She'd lost her husband a few weeks before and he worried about her mental stability. He decided it unfair that our mother had three children and his sister had none, so he falsified the birth certificate in order to give our brother to the other woman. He threatened the nurse on duty if she told anyone."

Someone in the crowd shouted out, "Who was that doctor?"

Chuck recognized the woman speaking from the gold mine. Thelma, the town gossiper wanted details, probably so she could go do more research.

"Let it be, Thelma. This ain't any of your business." Mutzi glared at the woman.

Marge nodded. "The poor woman carried the secret with her until the doctor and his sister both had passed. On her deathbed, she shared it with her granddaughter. If her granddaughter hadn't reached out to me, if I hadn't trusted a higher power to guide me, we'd never have known the name of our sibling, whose name was also on the report."

She turned and put a hand on Chuck's shoulder. "Milford Charles Hansen...you are our brother. Happy birthday."

The foreign words rolled around in Chuck's head. The clapping and cheering by the others was drowned by the confusion of the unexpected announcement.

Marge looked into his eyes. "Welcome home, Chuck."

Home. Sisters. Family. The notion stirred in Chuck's mind and flowed into his heart like molten lava, quenching the gaping cavity he'd struggled to satisfy most of his life. All the difficult twists and turns, disappointments and blessings, they were part of his journey to this place, to this family.

Mutzi stared at Chuck and grinned. "I knew there was something I liked about you." She gave him a high-five and let out a hoot. "By the way, you've got our mother's eyes." She looked at Marge. "Agree?"

"He sure does." Marge smiled.

The two formed a circle around Chuck and spoke as one, "Happy birthday, triplet."

"I can't believe this. It's overwhelming." He squeezed them tight, not wanting to let go. "Sorry, girls, I didn't get you anything."

Marge raised her eyes toward the sky. "I think someone else took care of that for all of us."

Rose Ellen squeezed in between Mutzi and Chuck. "I need one of those hugs, too. I'm your big sister, remember?"

Chuck laughed and turned to embrace her. "My big sister, Queen Rose. I can't believe I get to be part of this family. Do you think you can handle having a brother?"

"Sure. We've got plenty of love to go around." Rose Ellen winked. "But we'll always be The Dahlonega Sisters."

The End

Delightful venues in and around Dahlonega

The Fudge Factory candy store
http://dahlonegafudgefactory.com/

Dahlonega General store https://dahlonegageneralstore.com/

Giggle Monkey Toys https://www.gigglemonkeytoys.com/

Woody's Barber Sh91 N Park 2062 Public Square

Gustavo's Pizza 16 Public Square S
https://www.facebook.com/gustavospizza/

Dahlonega Gold Museum http://dahlonega.org/historic-downtown-4/dahlonega-gold-museum

Dahlonega Visitor Center 135 Park

PJ Rusted Buffalo Leather Store 98 Public Square N

Dahlonega Community House 111 N Park St

Shenanigan's Irish Pub http://www.theshenaniganspub.com/

Georgia Wine and Oyster Bar, 19 Chestatee St

The Smith House https://smithhouse.com/

Montaluce Estates & Winery http://montaluce.com/

University of North Georgia https://ung.edu/

Connor Community Garden Corner of N Chestatee and Warwick Sts

Consolidated Gold Mine https://consolidatedgoldmine.com/

Other venues mentioned outside of Dahlonega

Gibbs Gardens, Ballground, GA 30107
https://www.gibbsgardens.com/

Note: Magical Threads is a fictional location.

There are hundreds of other interesting places in and around Dahlonega that deserve to be mentioned, but space does not allow. The Dahlonega Sisters may have mentioned these locations in their stories. I apologize if I have omitted any. It was not intentional.

Acknowledgements

Writing often is a solo project. While I spend hours staring at my laptop screen, listening to my characters take my on their journey, and scripting their story into a novel, my supportive husband works alone outside in the yard attacking intrusive dandelions, tending his tomato garden, and filling the ever-empty bird feeders.

I know it's hard for him during rainy days and winter months when he tires of reading westerns, watching sports reruns, and walking the hall to complete his seven miles indoors. He tries hard to have patience as he waits for me to disengage from the computer as I craft one last sentence, blog post, or email. Bless you for putting up with me.

Much like the meticulous landscaping my hubby nurtures, my novel requires a great deal of fastidious enriching. Whether it's weeding out nonsense which doesn't belong, filling holes in my plots, or recognizing the difference between poetic allies and invasive nemeses, I need the help of critique groups, writing partners, and encouraging friends.

To the members of the Round Table Writers I extend my gratitude for enhancing my scenes, encouraging my writing, and being an available sounding board at the drop of an email. My short stories, novel chapters, and newsletter articles are always better hearing your critiques.

I thank my dear friends, Rose Ellen Koutsobinas and Denise Judd, for always being just a text or phone call away when I'm frustrated, happy, or need to lean on you.

To my dear Juliette Low Girl Scout sisters, I thank you for your help as beta and proof readers, the decades of loving friendship, and your continuous encouragement throughout my journey.

To my brother and sister-in-law, Bob and Lana Hootselle, and my daughter, Laura, thank you for your attention to detail as you proofed my manuscript for misspelled words, missing quotations and whatever else slipped past me.

Thank you to everyone who believed in me and supported my efforts in any way. You're terrific.

A Note to Readers

Thank you for reading *The Dahlonega Sisters, Veins of Gold*. This is the second book of the series. If you enjoyed the visit and haven't read *The Dahlonega Sisters, The Gold Miner Ring* you can find it at http://TheDahlonegaSisters.com

These charming women hope you will watch for their third book

The Dahlonega Sisters, Golden Adventures.

I hope the playful, light-hearted stories bring you as much joy as I have writing them.

I'd love to hear from you. Drop me a line at authordianemhow@gmail.com

Visit my blog at http://authordianemhow.com

Always in search of the positive side
Writing Silver Linings

Diane M How

ABOUT THE AUTHOR

Diane M. How is the author of the women's fiction series, *The Dahlonega Sisters*, which takes place in the historical gold rush town of Dahlonega, Georgia. The first of the series, *The Gold Miner Ring*, went to press in 2019. She also published a memoir, *Peaks and Valleys*, and more than twenty-five of her award-winning short stories and poems are available in numerous anthologies.

She is a member of the Missouri Writers Guild, St. Louis Writers Guild, and St. Louis Publishers Association. Diane is the treasurer of Saturday Writers, a non-profit organization with more than one-hundred members.

When Diane isn't writing, she enjoys walking five miles a day, reading, and visiting casinos with her husband of forty-nine years. She and her daughter have been weaving baskets for more than thirty years and are members of the Missouri Basket Weaver's Organization.